Unexpected Treasure

Billionaire Bachelors – Book Eight

Melody Anne

Printed and published in the United States of America.
Published by Gossamer Publishing Company
Editing by Nicole and Alison
Cover art by Trevino Creative
Salt Lake City, Utah

For creative purposes, the author has taken the liberty of altering California's smoking laws in this book. She understands that the laws changed in the mid- to late 1990s, and she hopes that none of her readers will rush out to Santa Catalina Island and light up at a bar.

ISBN-13 978-0615859224

ISBN-10: 0615859224

Dedication

This book is dedicated to Cindy Flory. Without you, the lost Andersons would have never been. Thank you for sharing your dream with me, for trusting me to make it into a story, and having the faith that I would do it right. I truly hope you like this next chapter in the Anderson Family. May you and your family continue to dream big.

Note from the Author

The Andersons are back, and I'm so happy about that. I've missed Joseph and George and all their meddling. I don't know how many people know this, but The Lost Andersons came about because one of my fans, Cindy Flory, had a dream that Joseph and George were sitting around the table when they saw a newspaper article with a picture of a man who looked just like them.

She took the time, wrote her dream down and sent it to me, and I was inspired. I was so completely impressed. Most of the prologue is from her dream. I made a couple of changes, but not a lot. I loved her dream from beginning to end. That is why you now have Richard, whom I hope you will love as much as you've loved Joseph and George.

If you haven't read about the Andersons yet, you can start here — no background reading is required. But you shouldn't miss out on the rest of this boisterous family. The story all begins with Joseph Anderson, who wants his children married and producing children. The first book in the series is free on all e-book sites if you want to give it a try.

Thank you to all of those who make my job so wonderful: my brother-in-law, Jeff, who is the world's best assistant and helps me out seven days a week; my designer and editor, Nikki, who deals with my crazy 2 a.m. demands; my newest editor, Alison, who is a genius and is now going through my entire collection; my sister Patsy, who is always willing to give me a hand; my Aunt Linda, who keeps my house from falling apart; Ray White, who gave my daughter an amazing graduation party so that I could still write and not feel like the world's worst mother; my children, whom I do all of this for. I don't say it enough, but my husband, who will give me foot rubs for no reason at all, hold me when I need to cry, cook for me at midnight, and tell me to put the laptop away so he can hold me. And a big thank-you always, always, always, my fans!! I love you!!

Writing takes a team, and I am the luckiest woman in the world to have a very supportive group of friends, family, and fans around me to make sure I am able to do what I love so much.

I hope you enjoy and love The Lost Andersons!!

Melody Anne

Books by Melody Anne

BILLIONAIRE BACHELORS

*The Billionaire Wins the Game

*The Billionaire's Dance

*The Billionaire Falls

*The Billionaire's Marriage Proposal

*Blackmailing the Billionaire

*Runaway Heiress

*The Billionaire's Final Stand

*Unexpected Treasure

BABY FOR THE BILLIONAIRE

+The Tycoon's Revenge

+The Tycoon's Vacation

+The Tycoon's Proposal

+The Tycoon's Secret

+The Lost Tycoon – **May 2014**

RISE OF THE DARK ANGEL

-Midnight Fire – Rise of the Dark Angel – Book One

-Midnight Moon – Rise of the Dark Angel – Book Two

-Midnight Storm – Rise of the Dark Angel – Book Three

Surrender

=Surrender – Book One

=Submit – Book Two

=Seduced – Book Three – **September 2013**

=Scorched – Book Four – **January 2014**

Melody Anne

Prologue

"I can't believe the way the grandchildren are growing like weeds. Little Jasmine is already fifteen, and boy, is she a beauty," Joseph said.

Sitting on the back deck with the morning sun streaming down upon them, Joseph and his brother George were enjoying light breakfast pastries and coffee while catching up on news about the kids and their week.

"I know, Brother. Little Molly is ten years old now. It feels like it was only yesterday that Trenton was fighting tooth and nail not to get married and settle down, and now he and Jennifer have a beautiful family with two kids. Not to mention their rowdy dog, Scooter, and feisty cat, Ginger."

"Don't forget that dang goose. Last time I was there, the rascal got me right in the tush. I need to take my hunting rifle with me the next time that I visit," Joseph threatened.

"If you'd just bring him some cracked corn like I do, he wouldn't chase after you," George said, not even attempting to hide his amusement.

"I'm not bribing a damn bird, and I'm certainly not running from one!"

"Ah, simmer down, Brother. I have a feeling the goose won't be the *end* of you — it's not as if you have a fundamental problem here, and you haven't hit bottom. So forget that cheeky critter and put the incident *behind* you" he guffawed, gleeful at making Joseph the butt of his joke. He tended to go a lot over the top when he found something so amusing.

Joseph mumbled something very unbrotherly under his breath, but he let go of his wrath against both George and the animals at his nephew's home. He had far more important issues to discuss, such as what they were going to eat that night.

"What are the plans for today?" George asked. "With Katherine and Esther out shopping, we can sneak away. I'm sick of golfing. Why don't we race go-karts again? That was a thrill."

"I think you're trying to kill me off, George. You slammed me against the wall the last time we went," Joseph huffed.

"You're acting like an old man, Joseph. We still have lots of life left in these old bones."

"True, George, very true. Fine. I'll give go-kart racing another try, though I hope that these old bones don't become these old *broken* bones. Let's see how many of the grandchildren we can gather up to go with us."

The men continued their morning meal as George pulled out the newspaper and flipped to the business section. Though George's son Trenton was now in charge of Anderson and Sons Incorporated, George still liked to keep up on what was going on in the Seattle area.

Joseph looked up just in time to see George gasp for air, his face white. Frozen with fear for a few endless seconds, Joseph felt his legs finally start working again and he jumped up to help his brother.

"George! What's wrong? Are you choking? Is it your heart? Speak to me, Brother," he urged as he leaned over to see what he could do. They'd had enough health scares to last them a lifetime and Joseph didn't think he could handle another near-death experience in his beloved family.

Just as Joseph began moving to race for the phone, George gestured wildly at the newspaper. Joseph stopped in his tracks and read the largest headline and subheadline on the page: "Billionaire buys flailing computer tech firm: Richard Storm sells East Coast shipping business, brings thousands of jobs to Seattle."

It wasn't the article that had Joseph turning as white as his brother. It was the photograph of a man who appeared to be their age — and who looked almost identical to the two of them, just a different hairstyle, some added wrinkles around the eyes, and a short beard covering his face.

"What is this?" Joseph gasped as he sank down in the chair next to George.

"I don't know. The picture just startled me — that's all. I'm sure it's nothing." George tried to reason it away, but he couldn't stop staring at the still eyes of the man gazing into the camera. It was like looking into a mirror.

"Well, read the dang thing," Joseph nearly shouted as he regained his voice. He pointed to a paragraph in the middle of the first column.

"Storm, who was born in Seattle, moved to the East Coast with his adoptive parents when still a baby. He says he owes his hard-work ethic to his father, who was a doctor in Seattle for 25 years before moving his medical practice to Portland, Maine. Storm was orphaned at age 18, when his parents died in a boating accident, and he used his modest inheritance to become a shipper of historic relics, mainly hard-to-find European artifacts from the 15th century. By the time he turned 30" — the newspaper gave a date — "he was worth more than $10 million — almost $60 million in today's dollars — and he continued to increase his fortune dramatically. Storm is a now a billionaire several times over."

"He was born here on the same day as we were? This can't be a coincidence."

"Let me keep reading."

"Go on then," Joseph said, still looking at the picture.

"Apparently, he married young, had five children — four boys and one girl — and then their mother left them. He's made the move here because he feels it's the right thing to do for his family."

"We need answers, and I want them now, George."

"I couldn't agree more."

The two men went inside to Joseph's large den and looked through the bookcase containing old family albums. When they came upon the album from the year they were born, they sat with it in front of the fireplace.

Less than an hour later, both men were speechless with shock. Richard Storm's adoptive father was the same man who'd delivered Joseph and George. Their mother even had notes in the album about her doctor, saying how kind he was and how sad she felt that he and his wife were unable to have children.

Only one conclusion appeared likely. This doctor must have seized the opportunity to give his wife a child, too desperate to care about the consequences of ripping another family apart.

"This man, Richard, may very well be our brother," George gasped as he gazed at the pictures of their mother holding them for the first time.

"But how is it possible she had a third child without realizing it?" Joseph countered.

"You know how different times were back then, Joseph. They didn't have ultrasounds, and Mother suffered complications during delivery. She'd lost a lot of blood and they had to put her under. Dad wasn't in the room — back then, fathers didn't belong there. The only other person in the room with the doctor was his nurse, who also happened to be his wife.

11

They could have easily seen the third child and taken the opportunity to create their own family. Why else would they have moved away so suddenly?"

"I just can't imagine that happening."

"That's because, if this is true, we have a brother out there we've missed knowing, and our mother has a child she never knew," George said, overtaken by sadness.

"One thing I know for sure — we need to meet this man and find out if he really is family."

"But what do you think that will do to him, Joseph? We would cause upheaval in his life, change everything that he believes about himself and his loved ones," George said. "Let's try to be reasonable."

"Can you honestly do nothing but stand by when a man who may be our kin is so close by? He has children, George, and they are most likely our nephews and our niece. We have to find out the truth, even if it's a painful one."

"You're right, Joseph. Of course you're right. I just don't know whether our visit will be a welcome one to this man. Heck, we know nothing about him. What if the man who could be our brother is a terrible person?"

"He can't be terrible, George. No matter what his birth certificate says, he's an Anderson, and Andersons are good people," Joseph said with confidence.

"Right you are, Joseph. Well, you know what this means, don't you?"

"Of course I do. Go-kart racing is off the schedule today. It looks like it's time to pay a visit to Richard Storm."

"I'll grab my hat. You lead the way brother; I'm right behind you."

The two men walked out the door, climbed into Joseph's Mercedes and made their way to the new Storm Corporate offices. Expectant smiles spread across their faces as they neared their destination. Granted, it would be heartbreaking to learn they had a brother they hadn't had the pleasure of growing up with. But still, if it were true, they were now blessed with a whole line of family members to get to know.

Joseph grinned, thinking of all those first-rate great-nieces and -nephews. More and more babies on the horizon and potential love matches to make.

Chapter One
Two years earlier

"Do any of you have any idea of what this is about?"

"Not a clue. It seems the old man has got something up his keister again. I haven't gone to bed yet from yesterday. I seriously considered not showing up."

"You may as well stop complaining about it, because you know how father gets. You don't want your precious trust fund cut off, now, do you?"

"Shut up, Brielle. You're the one who'd be hurting if you lost Daddy's money."

"All of you should shut up before the old man walks in. The more compliant we are, the sooner our family reunion can end, and the quicker we can get on with our lives."

"That's very good thinking, Lance. I know how important it is for you to run from my presence."

The five young bickerers turned in surprise to find their father standing in the doorway. Richard had to quickly disguise the sadness in his eyes. This wasn't the time to coddle his children, who, though grown up, were thoroughly spoiled. It was time to do what he should have done years ago, before it was almost too late. He didn't have much time left, and he feared that his kids would never change if he didn't act now.

Would they even care that the doctor had given him the grim diagnosis of only three years to live? At this point, he doubted they would. It saddened him to no end how much he had failed them — and he was certain that his failures as a parent had caused the distance among them all.

"Fine, you heard us complaining. We're sorry, Dad, but we haven't all been together in one room in years, so what's the big emergency?" Richard watched as his youngest child, Brielle, walked to the liquor cabinet and poured herself a scotch. She was only twenty-four years old, but she had so much bitterness inside her.

Why shouldn't she? Their mother had walked out on all of them, but Brielle was the only one who couldn't remember her — she'd only been three at the time. It made her feel as if she'd really missed out the most. Lance had vague memories, as he had been five, but Tanner, Ashton and Crew remembered the most. The kids were all two years apart, his ex-wife having produced them almost on a strict schedule.

Soon after Brielle was born, Suzanne was done being a mother and left them without ever turning back around. Richard had been too busy for years to date another woman, and when he'd tried, it had always been disastrous, since he'd been too exhausted to put forth any real effort. Eventually, he'd just given up.

He'd been wealthy and worked long hours to become even richer, leaving the children with nannies during the day. Yet he'd felt guilty enough to stay home in the evenings and on the weekends so he could spend as much time as possible with his offspring.

It was only when they'd gotten older that he'd started working even longer hours, and that's when they'd begun to drift away from him. He just hoped it wasn't too late to reverse the damage.

Now, here he stood in a room with grown children ranging in ages from twenty-four to thirty-two, and he didn't like them. He loved them, as he always would, but they'd become selfish and spoiled, and even worse — entitled.

"You've all been cut out of my will and I'm freezing your trust funds."

Richard watched as, slowly, each of his children turned toward him with varying expressions of disbelief. Of course it was Crew who finally cleared all expression from his face as he stood taller and faced his father.

"Do you care to elaborate?"

"My parents were hard workers their entire lives. They built not only one medical practice, but two.

16

They scrimped and saved, and gave me a good education. When they passed, I was devastated, but I took my inheritance and I created something both of them would be proud of. Unfortunately, I've pampered and indulged the five of you, making you think that life is nothing more than one big party, and that you deserve to be handed everything on a silver platter. Well, that stops today. As I've just said, you've been cut out of my will. Your trust funds are frozen, and your credit cards canceled —"

"You can't do that!" Ashton shouted.

"I can and I have. You can leave the room now and be on your way, or you can hear me out."

None of them budged, and Richard made sure to look each child in the eye. He refused to back down this time, no matter how many tears Brielle shed, or how convincing the group charmer, Tanner, tried to be. He would lose his children forever if he didn't stand firm and show them that life was about so much more than what they'd made it.

"You haven't really given us a choice other than to listen to you, have you? Is this your way of saying you need some attention? You could have just scheduled a lunch date," Lance said, trying to make a joke, but the anxiety in the room allowed no break in the tension.

"You always have a choice, Lance. It's your decision whether to make the right one or not. I'm really sorry you feel that way, though. It honestly breaks my heart. We were once a tight-knit family, laughing together, speaking often, *living* our lives. I don't know where I went wrong, but somewhere

17

along the way, you got lost, and now I'm allowing you to find yourselves again. I hope you do."

"OK, OK," Brielle said with a roll to her eyes. "What is this journey you want us to take?"

"I'm glad you asked, Peaches," he replied, reverting to the nickname he'd given her at birth because of the sun-kissed color of her hair, which was as stunning as the beginning rays of a sunset. Her deep-blue eyes widened at the use of the name he and her brothers had always called her. Somehow along the way they had stopped.

Brielle pulled herself together and looked back at her father with rage evident in her now-narrowed eyes. "I haven't been *Peaches* in fifteen years, Dad, but if you want to reminisce about the 'good' old days, then I'll go ahead and play your game."

The sarcasm and scorn pierced Richard to the heart.

"I've sold the family business. I've decided it's time for a fresh start, and I've chosen to do it on the West Coast. There is nothing in Maine to hold me any longer, and I'm tired of the tourist season. I've just finalized the paperwork on a failing computer tech firm, and I plan to turn it around. Doing that gave me an idea for the five of you."

Richard waited for it to sink in that his shipping empire was now gone. He knew Lance would be the most upset, as he'd been the one who'd invested the most time in the corporate offices. Richard missed those days when Lance, still in high school, was eager to learn all he could by his father's side.

Once the boy had left for college, then graduated, that interest had waned, and he acted as if he were just waiting to take over the business, but no longer eager to put in the effort. In the last several years, he'd become as spoiled as his siblings, but Richard, looking forward to a comfortable retirement, had still entertained a hope that the boy would one day take the reins. Now, that wasn't going to happen for his youngest son.

"Can this be reversed?" Lance's voice was strained with the amount of control he had to exert to keep his temper.

"No." Richard didn't elaborate.

"The business was supposed to be mine."

"Then you should have taken pride in it. You should have proved to me that you deserved a stake in the family business. I had hoped to pass it to you one day, but as of right now, you are unworthy to take the reins of any business of mine."

Another son broke in. "Don't you think that's a bit harsh, Father?"

"No, I don't, Crew. And you are no different from your brother. None of you has worked for an honest dollar, and I would rather see my funds passed down to people who can appreciate them than leave them to you with the way you've been acting. You have time to figure this out — well, time for now, at least."

"What is that supposed to mean — *for now*?" Tanner asked.

Richard took a calming breath. It wasn't yet time to tell his children of his prostate cancer. The doctor said he'd done all he could do. Of course, they would keep trying, but his doctor was also a good friend, and he'd warned Richard to get his affairs in order with his grim prognosis. *Three years.*

"Nothing, Tanner. You just need to pay attention. I want you to prove yourselves, make something of your lives. You are more than these spoiled brats I see before me right now."

"How are we supposed to do anything if we have no money? What do you want us to do to *prove* ourselves?" Tanner asked, throwing his hands into the air in exasperation.

"That's the smartest question you've asked me so far," Richard said with a smile before pausing to gaze at each one of his children. A glimmer of hope filled him at the fighting spirit he saw in each of them. "I have purchased five more failing businesses. You can fight amongst yourselves to choose which one you want to run. I have created a sufficient budget for you to do what needs to be done to bring the companies back into profitability. If you do this, and do it well, only then will I reinstate your inheritance. If you fail, you will be on your own."

"Well, what if your idea of a successful business is different from what our idea would be?" Ashton asked.

"When you truly feel success for the first time in your life, you will know what it is. You've never earned that badge of honor before. You'll learn now, one way or the other. I'm done explaining this. You may come see me when you're ready."

Setting down the folders of the five businesses he'd purchased, he noticed that none of the kids jumped up to see what the choices were. He knew they would, though. On the off chance they didn't, it would break his heart, but he would stay true to his word and cut them off. They would either make it, or not. What their decision would be was now out of their hands.

Richard walked from the room, his children bolting after him, trying to chase him down. Though he hadn't let them see the burden weighing on his shoulders, the conversation had hurt him in ways he couldn't begin to describe. He knew he was taking a huge gamble, but what other option had there been?

If he didn't kick his children out of their nest eggs, they'd never learn how to fly, never take pride in a true victory. He could end up losing them forever, but he already felt as if they were so incredibly self-absorbed that their only connection with their family was through blood. Richard had faith that his children would soon find their wings — they'd find their way back to him — and to each other. Only then would he be able to rest in peace.

Closing the door to his study in his children's faces, he looked down at the framed picture of his parents sitting in its special place on his desk. His mother's eyes were filled with joy as she cuddled him close to her heart. He was only six months old at the time, and it had taken his parents so long to have him that they'd doted on him his entire life.

Still, they'd taught him the core values that made him who he was today. He'd always worked hard, earned everything he'd ever striven for and appreciated the life he'd been raised to lead. He'd gotten lazy with his own children, but he knew it wouldn't be too late. He just had to have faith and stick with the plan.

They would all take it one day at a time, and then a week at a time. If he tried to think past that, it became too overwhelming. He had always protected his children, which he was still doing, just in a more *tough love* sort of way. He was determined that they *would* appreciate this, and him, someday.

Richard smiled as he thought back to their priceless expressions of rage and shock. They wouldn't be appreciating him anytime soon; that was for certain.

Chapter Two
Present day

Enjoying the fresh morning sun and gentle sea breeze, Crew Storm stood in front of his resort and smiled. Never would he admit to his father how good he felt, how much more alive, strong and happy he'd become since taking on the monumental task of refurbishing an oceanfront resort on exotic Catalina Island.

He couldn't give the man too much encouragement or he'd go on meddling in all of their lives from here on out. However, Crew did feel great. Maybe he'd cave and give the old man just a small thank-you. It was the least he could do since his father had put him on the right path. For a while, Crew had been lost, but that was a thing of the past, and now he only looked straight ahead.

In the last two years, Crew had truly grown up, and because of that he was rising to the top, learning how to fight for what he wanted, and he had

23

discovered that he wasn't one to back down from a challenge. Pride billowed up inside him as he turned to look at his finished project.

When he'd pulled the file for the resort, all he'd felt was extreme anger, resentment, and a determination to do the opposite of what his father wanted. It had all been nothing more than a game, and it was one that he had to win. He had planned on doing the bare minimum, getting his trust fund back, and never speaking to his dad again. What a fool he had been.

Now...now that had changed. Crew felt like a whole new man. It was about more than beating his old man — it was about taking pride in accomplishing a great task and feeling the satisfaction of victory over himself.

He'd completed a task many others would have failed at, and it felt incredible to see the resort in all her former glory — better than her former glory, in fact. She was a shining jewel, ready to bring Catalina Island back to the ultimate vacation destination. In the nineteen-thirties Catalina Island had been at her heyday, the ultimate place to spot the stars, and to vacation like a king. This resort was the beginning of reinventing the thirties with a twenty-first-century bang.

Crew had always been tenacious, never willing to back down from a challenge. His father said it was because he came from good stock. And his dad seemed to have the Midas touch. Crew found it a thrill to know he was making smart choices, and he had a better relationship with his father than he'd ever thought he'd have again.

His father had thrown him and his siblings out to fly or to die, and changed all their lives forever. Never before had he looked himself in a mirror and felt shame, but after the first six months of sweating it out pounding nails into wood on the broken-down resort, he'd woken up one day to realize he was a different man. After a year, he'd called his father to apologize.

Now, finally, he was ready to open his new resort, and he was proud for people to walk through her doors. Yes, this thing of beauty before him couldn't be called anything but a woman, because her curves were smooth, her lines flawless, and she'd been transformed by his blood, sweat and…well, not tears, but she'd gotten everything else she could out of him.

As he gazed in adoration at the sleek and glistening entryway, he felt a pang in his heart. He knew to sell her would be bittersweet, but that was the deal. Get the business up and running, turn it around, and then make a profit.

It wouldn't be easy, but a smile flitted across his lips when he thought of doing it all over again. His father had laid down the law, setting the ultimate challenge, and the old man had won, because Crew was changed forever now, and a man his dad could be proud of. Crew had discovered what he excelled at, and he would embrace that gift, even if he left a piece of himself behind each time he left the old and ventured on to a new project.

The old resort had been in shambles, the corporation going bankrupt, and it was walking away, leaving the place to fall into the sea. She wasn't tall, only ten stories high, but each floor had a theme, and each room was fit for royalty. Crew's absolute favorite floor was the flamboyant thirties. He had to dedicate a floor to the year the resort had originally opened, of course.

The wide hallways were decorated with fine pieces of art and vintage antiques he'd uncovered in his high-powered hunting. Fresh flowers decorated delicate tables; the colorful bouquets would draw the eye of every customer who stepped from the cherry-wood-lined elevators. Hand-fashioned carved railings led up the wide staircases, and the walls were painted in soft golden hues. Dazzling chandeliers glowed in the center of each room and down the grand corridors.

He'd poured his entire soul into the place, and he wanted his clientele to walk through the doors and instantly feel as if they were in a luxurious wonderland. His staff would treat each and every one like the most important guest in the building, and they all would want to return over and over again.

He'd hired only the best cooks, and his restaurants would soon be famed for tantalizing entrées and enticing ambience. A small theater room was decorated with dark colors, soft lighting and red velvet curtains above a stage where live bands and professional vocalists would perform. The resort planned to cater to its guests' every whim, wanting no one to feel the need to step outside onto the island for anything except the abundant gifts of nature.

Half of the rooms faced an exquisite stretch of the Pacific Ocean, and half faced the inner workings of the island. Crew's preference, of course, was the water, but there were many who would want to open their French doors and step out on the balcony to watch the entertainment below of a town that played hard, and never stopped moving.

The price tag at his resort wasn't cheap, but the clientele he attracted wouldn't bat an eyelash. They would pull out their wallets, open them willingly, and, in turn, they would get to experience a once-in-a-lifetime vacation.

A stay on his small corner of Catalina would have them floating back home, dreaming in vivid color with digital animation where before they arrived it was only in black-and-white Claymation. The longing for a return, for paradise regained, would begin the minute they left the resort.

A burst of adrenaline caused Crew's stomach to tense as he took a stroll around the outside of the building. His staff was busy, doing all the last-minute preparations needed for a successful grand opening. As the small island awoke to a new day, he awaited the twelve o'clock hour — when the resort doors would open to the public for the first time in ten years.

Though she wouldn't be his for too long, when he finally proved her a success, the months he did have her would be glorious, and he would set the standard for the staff to follow. When he finally sold, under the deal with his father, it would be only to someone who would give the Catalina Couture Resort the same tender loving care that he did.

As he stepped back inside, he was pleased that his marbled floors gleamed, too clean to admit a single germ on their pristine surface. The detailed stained glass sparkled in brilliant colors, the flowers majestic fragrance filled the room, and the Italian granite counters shone. The last of the edibles were being put away in the kitchens, and the final inspection was being performed on the rooms. His project was a work of beauty and she was soon to open her doors.

Chapter Three

Gazing at the man walking from the resort, Haley felt her blood racing as she firmed her shoulders and gave herself a pep talk, which sadly, wasn't unusual for her. Though she put forth the appearance of a woman who had it all together, she didn't know how she pulled it off.

"I can't do this," she whispered to herself, then felt anger well up inside. She was tired of backing down, tired of being afraid of rejection. She wasn't the horrid being that her evil grandparents had continually made her believe she was. She was a strong, beautiful woman who could speak to a handsome stranger without fear and trembling.

As a matter of fact, Crew Storm didn't feel like a stranger to her, because she'd researched the heck out of the man. She needed to know him inside and out if

29

she were to ask him what she was about to — that was, *if* she didn't chicken out.

Her college professor had suggested a summer assignment just for her. She was to approach a stranger and ask for a date. It didn't need to be anything more than a ten-minute coffee date, but she still had to ask a man out. He felt this would help her to get over her fears. At first she'd thought he'd gone mad, but as the idea had sunk in, she realized he was right. She could and *would* ask a man on a date. She just needed someone to teach her how to do it properly.

Why had she taken the human-sexuality course in the first place? It wasn't as if it were going to be a part of her career. She was an archaeology major, eager to explore the ruins of ancient civilizations. Living people were trouble; Haley wanted to focus on the dead. Or did she?

She knew why she'd taken the course. She was tired of being afraid of men. It was ridiculous to make it to the age of twenty-six and still be a virgin. She'd been infatuated with a man on her college campus for two years and yet she couldn't work up the courage to ask him out on a date.

Now, she was on Catalina Island with a free two-week stay in an exclusive resort, and it was the perfect time for her to learn how to be a consummate seductress. If she could convince this man to teach her, she could go back to her college and ask the guy of her dreams out to lunch — maybe even dinner, if she worked up enough courage.

Haley watched cautiously as Crew Storm checked every inch of his resort, not the slightest possible flaw invisible to his fastidious blue eyes. If there was something wrong, he would find it. The man's strides were long and powerful, as if every step he took had a purpose, and there was no wasted energy in his movements.

He was tall — intimidatingly tall — standing a few inches over six feet, making her feel almost dwarflike at five foot six. Working on the island had obviously been good to him. His tan was a creamy golden color, making the blue of his eyes glow from beneath his thick, dark lashes.

Without a doubt, however, his hair was his best feature — just long enough for a woman to run her fingers through, then grab a handful and guide his mouth in the direction she most desired.

Although she hadn't spoken the words aloud, Haley's face flamed; she looked around, afraid someone nearby could actually *hear* her thoughts. What was wrong with her? She didn't want to appreciate Crew Storm's beauty; she wanted to hire him.

She could do this. When she'd found out she'd won the dream vacation, she'd hopped on her computer and researched all she could about the island and the resort. She'd found out the owner was an eligible bachelor and babe magnet. He had a new woman on his arm every week and was exactly the kind of man she needed to teach her how to be what she wanted to be.

"Do not chicken out!" she snarled under her breath before stepping from the shadows and making her way down the beautiful slate walkway. She'd parked around the corner, since the resort wasn't open yet and management wasn't allowing in cars, trying to prevent an early mob.

Though she should be trying to be a femme fatale at the moment, she was woefully underdressed in her loose linen blouse and jean capri pants. She'd been in school for the past three years, plus working part-time at a small stationary store and she never had the energy to dress up or worry about clothes. It had taken her five years of therapy to work up the courage to go to college in the first place, or she would have been finished with her education by now.

Though she'd received a large inheritance when she was nineteen, she hated using the money because her grandparents hadn't wanted her to have it. They'd just never made a will, and because she was their only heir, the money had come to her. She was sure that if they'd taken the time to designate beneficiaries, they would have left it all to their precious birds rather than to her.

Still, there were times it was necessary for her to dip into her substantial funds. This was one of those times.

It was now or never.

"Are you lost?" Haley stopped the shiver fighting to travel down her spine from just the deep timbre of his voice. Oh yes, she had chosen well. This man could teach her all she wanted to know. He was sex personified.

"No. I'm looking for you, Mr. Storm."

Nervous tension filled her as his gorgeous eyes gave her body the once-over. When they reached her face, she had the feeling that he'd checked her out and found her wanting.

Too bad!

She'd planned this down to the smallest detail, and she'd make him help her.

"And what can I do for you, miss?"

Oh, the promise in his tone was what women's wet dreams were made of. She knew he spoke to every woman this way. She'd studied him, read about how effortlessly he flirted — how women fell at his feet. With one snap of his fingers, females young and old were panting, their salivary glands in overdrive.

"Haley Sutherland," she said a little breathlessly as she stuck out her hand.

After a slight pause, he grasped her fingers and squeezed, then slowly lifted their entwined hands to his mouth and ran his lips across the top of her knuckles, his warm breath brushing over her skin.

"This!" Haley practically shouted as excitement filled her.

Crew's normal cool seemed to be shaken; he stared at her in confusion. The expression on his face was almost comical as he stood frozen with his lips only a couple of inches from her skin.

"I want you to teach me how to seduce someone. I have been reading about you, studying the way you flirt, how you can have any woman you want. I want you to teach me how to get a man, how to make him want me so much that he can't see straight, how to make him drop to his knees."

"Ummm…are you drunk?" Crew asked after a long pause as he dropped her hand and took a retreating step. Haley had no doubt he thought she was crazy. Perhaps she was at the moment.

However, now that she was warmed up, she couldn't hold back. She followed his steps, not realizing what she was doing until he bumped against the outside wall of his resort and her hand was pressed against his chest.

"I know this seems weird, and maybe I should have eased into it, but I am in love with a man who doesn't know I'm alive and my psych professor suggested that I ask him out as a way of getting over my fears, but I get all tongue-tied around him, which just can't happen. I want you to teach me how to make him want me — desire me — need me! I have money. Lots of it. I'll pay you any amount you want if you will agree to be my teacher."

Haley didn't feel a trace of fear as she gazed into Crew's eyes. All she felt was exhilaration. She knew he could do it — he could turn her from the wallflower she'd always been into a seductress who would get her man.

"Let me get this straight. You want to pay me to teach you how to seduce a man?"

"Yes!" she gasped, relieved he was starting to get it.

"I honestly don't know what to say." His tone of voice didn't alert her at all to what he was thinking.

"Say *yes*."

Chapter Four

Crew couldn't remember a time in his life when he'd been rendered speechless, not even when his father had given him and his siblings that horrendous ultimatum a couple of years earlier.

This wisp of a woman, who looked a bit too much like a teenage girl, was asking him to teach her how to be a seductress. If it were dark out, he'd think he was dreaming. Was she a kid, and was he being punked? Or was she a crazy person who'd escaped from a mental hospital?

Whoever she was, she couldn't be serious. Who walked up to a stranger and asked such a thing of them? Certainly not a rational person, someone with full brain functionality.

As he stalled to try to figure out how to make her go away, she pulled her hand back and leaned to her right, her other hand propping on her hip, giving him a glimpse of the curves beneath her baggy blouse. Her foot began to tap, and he noticed her slim ankles, and the smooth skin of her tanned shins.

Giving Ms. Haley Sutherland a bit more of a thorough evaluation, he decided she couldn't possibly be a teenager. There was a woman's body hiding behind all that fabric, and sparks were radiating in her misty eyes, such a pale color of green that they were almost translucent.

Her hair was tied back in a very sloppy bun, but tendrils of her long blond hair floated about her face. She was pretty, he decided, but obviously crazy, too, which could be a key reason this man she was in love with avoided her at all costs.

It was too bad, really, since she was enticing enough to drop a man to his knees if she knew how to put away the crazy talk and maybe choose another outfit. His inner thoughts amused him, and a smile broke free. He hated to disappoint any person of the female persuasion, but it looked as if this was one damsel in distress he wouldn't be able to help.

"Well, are you going to just stare at me all day, or are you going to give me an answer?" she huffed, then before he could say anything, she held up her hand. "And before you think I'm insane, I *guarantee* you, I'm not. I am just tired of sitting in a corner, tired of being this invisible person. This is one assignment that I'm determined to get an A on, even if it's not for credit. You wouldn't know what it's like to always be invisible, since you're gorgeous and wealthy and have women drooling over you, but I am all too aware. It's lonely and disappointing and I just want a new life for myself."

Crew held up his hand to cut her off. Man, could the woman talk, and talk, and talk. To his utter surprise, her babbling was actually getting through to him on some insane level in his brain. He was intrigued by her request.

How was he supposed to teach her how to catch a guy, though? It wasn't as if there were books out there on how to seduce a man. Or maybe there were. Hell, he didn't know. After all, he'd never had to learn the art of seduction. It just came naturally to him, he thought proudly.

"Why would you think I'd even consider doing such a thing?" he finally asked, surprised he was in fact leaning toward accepting her wacko proposal. He didn't have time for this. There was no way. He had a resort to run, and then to sell. When this project was safely locked in the hands of someone else, he had to start all over on his next project. He didn't have time for crazy females with even nuttier requests.

"Because I've learned about you. The way you flirt with women is simply effortless. If you teach me how to be one of those women you'd want to be with, then I know I can win my guy. He won't even know what hit him."

"How far exactly do you want this to go?"

"What do you mean?" By the innocent expression on her face, he could see she really had no clue of what he was talking about. With quick movements, he decided to show her.

In one smooth motion, his arms encircled her, and he backed her against the side of the resort, tucking them both into the shadows and bringing his face to within an inch of hers. The widening of her eyes and quick intake of her breath sent a surge of adrenaline warming his insides. Let her see what happens when she decides to play with fire. By the time he was done with his lesson, she'd run away before he had a chance to blink, and her ridiculous idea would be totally forgotten.

"Do you want me to teach you how to be a seductress, or teach you how to seduce? I can teach you many things, Haley, but believe me, I don't need to be paid for my lessons — at least not in cash."

When her cheeks flushed and her eyelids drooped, Crew was overwhelmed with the desire to kiss her. Since she'd be running away screaming in a few moments, he was debating on sampling her lips just one time. Just as he got ready to close the gap between them, her eyes widened and a huge smile spread across her face, causing him to lose his momentum.

What had just happened?

"Yes! That! That's what I want you to teach me. Oh, my gosh, I couldn't breathe for a second there as you were all sultry and sexy and pressing against me. It felt like my stomach was on fire and my heart was going a thousand beats a minute. Teach me how to do that same thing to Walker!"

The excitement bouncing from her was a real blow to Crew's ego, especially when she slid out from beneath his arms and danced in a little circle in front of him. But the wide-eyed innocence in her expression made him want to tuck her away and save her from herself.

"I can't do this."

For a split second her smile stayed in place, and then her face fell. He felt as if he'd just shot her favorite kitten. She was obviously crushed.

"I understand. I thought it was a long shot getting you to be my teacher, but a girl's got to try, right?"

Were those tears in her eyes? He hated feminine tears, hated the power they wielded. Everyone cried, so why did it make him feel like such a tyrant when a stranger shed a tear or two? Until a few minutes ago, he hadn't even known Haley Sutherland existed, so what did it matter if she was crying?

"I'm sorry, Haley. I really am, but I'm a busy man, and I don't know the first thing on how to teach this kind of…lesson. I'm sure you can find a good self-help book, though, one that will give you all the answers you need. They're publishing everything nowadays."

"I'm sure you're right, Mr. Storm. I appreciate your listening to me, and thinking about it, even if it was only for a second," she said, her eyes narrowing at the end of her sentence.

Without saying anything further, Ms. Haley Sutherland turned and walked away from him. He watched the sway of her curvy hips, and, stupidly, he wanted to shout out to her that she had a few moves already capable of seducing a man, but he knew that would be a mistake.

The farther away the crazy woman was, the quicker he'd be able to forget about her. Once she had turned the corner, he went back to admiring his resort, his achievement. Unfortunately, as the day progressed and his doors officially opened, one small woman and her ridiculous proposal remained on his mind.

He knew that the madness would pass soon enough.

*****

Haley walked away feeling defeated for about five minutes. Once she was out of sight of the resort, she turned back around and glared in the general direction of where she assumed Crew Storm was.

He was the only man she'd found *so far* who could teach her how to be the perfect seductress, but he wasn't the only man capable of teaching her. With relentless determination building inside, Haley walked to her car and looked at her paperwork. She was going to be staying in a tropical paradise in the summertime.

There were bound to be several single men staying at the luxury resort. At least one of them would take her up on her offer. With a smile, she drove to a small café where she could comfortably wait for the resort to open.

Looking around, she thought, *It's all or nothing*.

Haley's upbringing had been the stuff of horror. It had taken her years of therapy and then college to learn how wrong her grandparents had been in the way they'd treated her. The shame was on them for how they treated her and she shouldn't feel this much inadequacy. When they'd died and she inherited their money, it had felt not like a victory, but a burden.

40

Until now, she'd been unwilling to use her inheritance for anything other than her schooling, so she'd squirreled the money away, living cheaply while working on her bachelor's degree. Now, she was almost finished with her education, but her line of study wasn't doing much for her at this particular moment. She had a ways to go before she'd make a real living at it.

Some people might have thought her vain or irresponsible for rushing off on a quest to learn the art of love, but if they knew about the despair and utter loneliness of the childhood neglect she'd suffered, or about the many years of being picked on and feeling invisible, they'd probably have given her a pass. She wanted to reinvent herself, and nothing was going to stand in her way.

The spring term had just ended, and with studying for finals and excitement about her trip, she hadn't had a decent night's sleep in weeks, and she couldn't remember the last time she'd thought to feed herself something other than Ramen Noodles and Budget Gourmet. It would be nice to stay in the resort, where she could sleep in without fear of missing school, and eat at the press of a button.

Once her basic bodily needs had been taken care of, the hunt for a new guy to teach her what she wanted would be on. The perfect place to start would be the resort lounge. From her observations, slightly intoxicated men were far more willing to do the bidding of strange women.

After finishing her meal and noting the time, Haley drove back to the resort, surprised by the huge line of people parading down the quaint paths. Luckily, valet parking wasn't too busy, and she had to wait only about five minutes before a good-looking young man opened her car door.

"Sorry about the wait, Miss, but opening day has been busy. Are you staying with us tonight?"

"Yes I am, and the wait wasn't bad at all." She gave him a huge smile and was delighted when his cheeks flushed. Too bad he was so young — and so shy. She needed a man, not a boy.

"Um…just take this slip inside with you, and we'll be sure to bring your bags to your room," he stuttered, giving Haley confidence she didn't know she had.

"Thank you…," she said, pausing as she looked at his name tag, "…Sammy. You have a great day."

Life was already looking up. As she stepped inside the plush lobby of the resort, Crew was nowhere to be seen, but that was OK with her, because there were plenty of men to take his place.

As she looked around, she suddenly felt like sinking through the floor. This place was so far out of her league, she felt it was a sin to be standing on the magnificent floors. Though, she had seven figures in the bank, the clientele here spent that kind of money in a month, for vacation homes, expensive cars, and charity donations.

When her grandparents had died, a big chunk of their estate had been taken in taxes and payment on debts, but she still wouldn't complain at what she had. She could live comfortably on the interest alone if she chose, but she wouldn't be able to come to resorts such as this on the money in her bank account.

Beautifully dressed staff members were walking around the crowded lobby, carrying trays filled with eye-catching appetizers and full glasses of wine in honor of the grand opening. The lobby oozed elegance and perfection. Every last touch seemed to have been planned, down to the minutest detail.

Overwhelmed and hoping she hadn't made a mistake, Haley found she couldn't get her feet to move. She was underdressed and she stuck out like a sore thumb in the roomful of sophisticated people. Even the cleaning staff were dressed better than she was.

In every direction she looked, handsome men in hand-tailored suits were standing around chatting with other people also dressed to the nines, or leaning against the romantic railings lining the whimsical staircases.

This was a high-class place, one where even the floors stood out with their unique marble patterns, and she felt a thrill to be a guest. Not entirely a good thrill, but she refused to allow herself be too intimidated. Though she felt an intense impulse to turn around and run back outside, she fought it and was winning. She wasn't that girl who was allowed to associate only with the servants and certainly no one of any social standing, not anymore.

She wasn't living with her tyrannical grandparents — they were long gone. She had money, and she could go wherever she felt like going.

Still, her surroundings filled her with the overwhelming emotion of not being good enough. It was impossible to go through life on the outside, and then suddenly feel as if you were a part of the action. No matter how much was in her bank account, she knew who she was, and she just didn't fit in with this diamonds-and-caviar crowd. Refusing to cower, though, she raised her chin and squaring her shoulders, sauntered up to the granite-topped front desk, where a smiling woman greeted her.

"Welcome to the Catalina Couture Resort. We're delighted to have you on our opening day."

"Thank you," Haley replied as she reached into her purse for her identification and credit card. Though her room was free, she would definitely take advantage of the room service options. This was the vacation of a lifetime and she *was* going to enjoy every moment, even if she had to plaster a fake smile on her face.

"Your reservation is all set, Ms. Sutherland. I'll just have you sign right here, and our bellman will assist you to your room and explain about our services." With a smile that still betrayed a hint of awe, Haley thanked the woman, grateful for her genuine kindness that somehow settled her nerves, then followed a young man to the elevators, where he pushed the number for the tenth floor.

When she'd won this vacation, she hadn't thought she'd get the top floor. This was truly a cream-of-the-crop prize. She'd have a nice view of either the ocean or the island.

As they began the short journey up, Haley turned toward the kid assisting her. "Do you enjoy working here?"

His eyes glanced down, but not before settling a split second longer than usual at her chest as he replied. "We've only done training so far, but yes, this place is the *breast*...I mean...um...best!" he exclaimed; his face reddened and he stared at his shoes in mortification.

Haley could fully understand the poor kid's feelings. She had put her foot in her mouth more often than she cared to think about. Patting his shoulder, she waited for him to look up again, which he did with obvious reluctance.

"Don't worry about the slip. I do it often," she said with a kind laugh. *Well, not that particular slip, but...*

He breathed out a sigh of relief and his eyes practically worshipped her. If only she could speak to men she was attracted to as easily as she spoke to service employees. It was just that she felt closer to the workers, as if they were her kin, because she'd been raised by her grandparent's staff members.

"You have one of our larger suites, reserved for our VIP guests," the boy said as he stepped from the elevator. He escorted her a short distance down the hallway before sliding a card into a key slot and then holding the door open for her to walk in ahead of him.

"Perfect," Haley gasped as she glanced around the spacious living room area. The scent of roses drifted to her from the large bouquet on the coffee table — with a box of chocolates next to it. The furnishings were antique, matching much of the resort decor. Across the room, opening onto a private balcony, were ornate French doors displaying a spectacular ocean panorama.

At least if she couldn't find a man to teach her all she wanted to know, she'd spend two fabulous weeks in complete paradise. This room was too good to be true, and she hadn't even wandered into the bedroom yet.

The young bellhop began telling her about all the amenities of the resort: spa, gym, room service, lounges, and more. She didn't really care. She could learn all of that by looking through the catalog on the small desk in the corner.

She just wanted some food and a lot of sleep.

When he finished speaking, she handed him a nice tip and moved him toward the door. He smiled in delight before finally departing. Not wanting to wait for room service, Haley ripped into the box of chocolates, then walked to the small fridge and found a Coke.

Grabbing her sugary dessert, she carried them to the bedroom, where she smiled in pure happiness. The four-poster king-size bed was heaven on wooden feet. She ripped off her pants and shirt, dived onto the bed, and wriggled gleefully under the covers.

It didn't take her long to devour half of the box of chocolates and guzzle down the Coke. She knew she should at least get up and brush all the sugar off her poor teeth, but the feather pillows were calling her name.

With a sigh, she gave up the fight. Closing her eyes, she indulged in her first good nap in ages. How could she do anything other than relax while in such a fantastic place? Tonight, she needed to be fully alert when she went on the prowl.

Chapter Five

Haley awoke with a huge yawn, stretching her arms above her head until she grasped the headboard. She'd left the curtains open and she watched as the last rays of a spectacular sunset glowed through the huge open windows, a salty breeze blowing in from the Pacific Ocean.

A smile flitted across her face as she let go of the deep cherry wood and sat up. Her days of finals at school and planning her summer assignment had worn her out and she hadn't rested this well in what seemed like eons. She'd have to find out where Crew purchased his beds because the mattress was simply divine.

As a loud growl from her stomach interrupted her happy thoughts, Haley laughed, then bounded out of bed. She loved waking, finding herself in a whole new day — well, a whole new night, since it was beginning to get dark outside.

Rapidly moving to the bathroom, she stripped down and jumped into the oversized shower, moaning as the forceful jets did their job of fully waking her up and of washing the grime of the day down the drain.

Maybe it was time she dipped into her inheritance funds for more than her schooling; she had a feeling that after staying in such a nice place, it would be difficult to go back to her small apartment in Seattle. If she could transport this shower, it might not be *so* bad…

The brass fixtures and granite tile gleamed, and the beveled glass was crystal clear. The bathroom even had a separate beauty area with a dark velvet bench where she could sit if she wanted to apply makeup and do her hair. It wasn't her style to get done up, but maybe she should experiment, spend some more time on trying to look her best.

It was evident that Crew insisted on only the best, because the shampoo was amazing and the scent of peaches and mangoes drifted around her as suds enveloped her hair. Maybe there was something in aromatherapy — Haley was energized to face the night and Plan B in the seduction stakes.

Within an hour she was showered, dressed, and ready to seek out conversation and perhaps a bit of food, so she decided on the jazz bar inside the resort. And since Haley had worked a number of years in restaurants, she knew it was wise to make friends with the resort staff and especially the cooks. If you were friendly with them, tipped well, and sucked up a bit, you could eat so much better and get to try dishes no one else knew existed.

Anticipation hurried her movements. She tucked some cash into her pockets, along with her room key, then grabbed her small handbag. She preferred leaving it behind, but it had a couple of essential items she couldn't go without.

Ready to roll. She had a determined set to her mouth as she shut the suite door behind her and made her way toward the elevators. It was time to find a teacher.

The lobby was even busier now than when she'd arrived, with people speaking excitedly as they sat in the high-backed chairs circling small tables with stunning vases sitting atop them. The flowers had to be real, making her want to touch them to make sure, but she kept on moving forward, on a mission to find a friendly staff member to give her information. She wished she had the courage to sit down and join in a conversation with the other hotel guests, but she didn't at this point. Maybe soon...

Put a uniform on a person, and she could open up like a pirated book, but a man wearing a business suit like her grandfather had worn made her want to hide in the farthest corner. She was going to work on that —— even if it took her a while, as change often did, she'd eventually gain the courage to step outside her comfort zone.

Approaching the busy bar, she saw and heard an attractive musician playing soft music in the corner. His fingers caressed the keys of the grand piano, and several guests at nearby tables applauded when he finished a piece.

Hmmm. Those fingers showed promise.

Haley could picture herself sitting next to him on the bench, his chords washing over her as her own fingers drifted up his thigh. Whoa! Such thoughts weren't helping her. She had a mission — a mission to ask the man she liked back home out on a date — *not* to hit on every eligible bachelor in this place. All she needed was to find a man willing to give her some pointers, give her some confidence, teach her how to seduce the man she wanted.

So far tonight, luck was with her: she found an open bar stool at the back of the counter, a spot almost guaranteed, in her experience, to get the most attention from the bartender. Seeing an ashtray nearby, she knew this was where he'd sneak over when he had a few moments to drag in a couple puffs of nicotine.

"Good evening. What are you drinking?" he asked hurriedly, barely glancing at her. This, Haley was used to. *Story of my life.*

"How about you surprise me? You look like a man who knows how to make a good drink," she said with an open smile, and she pulled out her emergency cigarettes. She hated the smelly things, but she'd found they could be a great ice-breaker when she was with a smoker.

That gained his attention. He looked longingly at her thin white cigarette as she lit it with a flick of her cheap plastic lighter. Making sure she didn't inhale — she hardly wanted to start coughing all over the poor man — she took a shallow puff while waiting for him to reply.

"Ah, an adventurous woman. I like that," he said with a smile, showing he had one tooth missing in the corner of his mouth. It added character to his leathery cheeks.

Within a minute, he brought her a large layered cocktail with fruit on a stick. What fun!

"This here I call Marlin's special," he said with a chuckle. "Do you want to open a tab?"

"I'm assuming you're Marlin?" When he nodded, she continued. "Well, Marlin, that would be lovely. Do you need my credit card or room key?" When his eyes drifted to her dangling cigarette again, Haley remembered to take a puff, before catching his eye.

"I'm being so rude. Would you like one?"

Marlin looked around to be sure nothing needed to be done at his bar, and then held out his hand. "That would be great, and your room key is sufficient."

Gotcha! Haley thought. Yes, she knew how to speak to staff.

Within an hour Haley knew that Marlin had a wife he'd been married to for thirty years, two grown children, and two unexpected, but wanted, surprises. He'd moved to Catalina Island ten years earlier, and he was elated to be working at the Catalina Couture Resort, telling her it was the nicest bar he'd ever run. She had to agree with him there.

"Try this, honey," Marlin said as he placed a bowl of soup in front of her.

Haley didn't even bother asking what was in it. The intoxicating aroma made her stomach and her salivary glands sit up and take notice. With her first sampling, she couldn't repress an ecstatic groan.

"That there is a chef's special he only gives to the boss and staff. Don't ask what he puts in it. Ignorance is bliss," he said with a cackle.

"Can I get a bowl of that?" a man sitting two seats down asked as he eyeballed Haley's soup.

"Sorry, we don't serve food," Marlin told him. The man raised his brows as he looked from Marlin to the bowl of soup in front of Haley. He obviously didn't want to call Marlin a liar, but the evidence was right there.

"Um..." the man cleared his throat.

"Haley works here. She's just on break," Marlin lied with a perfect smile at the man, and Haley had to hide her giggle. Yes, she and Marlin were going to be great friends.

She fearlessly finished her bowl before reluctantly passing it back. It had took the edge off her hunger, but not taken it away. "Whatever his secret ingredients are, they are working for him. Thank you, Marlin. I know where I'm hanging out in the evenings from now on."

"I won't complain about that. You're quite a treat to visit with. How long are you staying with us?"

"Well, I have two weeks that I won for free, but really as long as it takes!" When his eyebrows rose in question, she laughed before filling him in. "I'm looking for a man to teach me how to be the perfect seductress."

Marlin's jaw dropped and he choked on his coffee. Haley wiped the spray from her cheek as he looked her in the eye, obviously trying to figure out whether she was pulling his leg or not. When she stared back, he finally roared with laughter.

"Well, I'd offer my services, but then my wife would chop my head off," he said between bouts of laughter.

"Oh, Marlin, I think you are way too much man for me to handle anyway," she said with a wink.

"You are sure good for my ego, honey. Now, tell me about your plans," he insisted as he grabbed another cigarette and leaned against the counter so their faces were close together.

"Well…" She hesitated. "My original plan was for your boss to teach me, but he isn't cooperating," she pouted.

Marlin's eyes widened for a second before he burst out laughing again. "Oh, Haley, I'm so very pleased I've met you. I have a feeling you're sure going to shake up things around here," he guffawed.

Was he making fun of her? Haley wasn't certain, but she had come too far to turn back now. "Tell me about him. How can I get Crew Storm to help me?"

Marlin looked down the bar, again making sure that his employees were doing their job and that his customers were all happy before he turned back to her and leaned in even closer.

"Crew is a good guy. Most places like this — kinda snooty, to tell you the truth — take one look at me and move on down the line. They want pretty young girls or studly young men to tend the counters,

54

figuring they'll draw in more people. They don't look at experience; all they care about is the way a person looks."

Sadly, Haley knew this was true.

"But not Crew. No siree. He doesn't mince his words, though. He asked me flat out what happened to my missing tooth. I told him I was young and got in a fight. You want to know what he asked then?"

"Yes," Haley said. She hadn't a clue.

"He asks if I won or not," Marlin said with a laugh. "I proudly told him the other guy went away without three of his teeth."

Haley burst into laughter as she looked at Marlin's gaping grin, but her amusement wasn't complete. She already knew that she would miss this man when she moved on. She could choose to just live here, but then she'd never finish her degree. She felt a little heartbreak over the inevitable: people always said they'd write, but then friendship would slowly fade into nothing.

She shook herself out of her melancholy. "Wow! You must have been surprised," she told Marlin.

"I knew as soon as he gave me that Crew Storm smile that he was a different kind of man — one of the good guys. He told me he'd both won and lost his own share of fights. Then, he got real professional and asked me what I could do to make this the best bar on the whole island. It took me a minute, then I just told him what I did best. He hired me on the spot, didn't even hesitate. He said he just got a feeling about people, and he could tell I was the right man for the job."

"How long have you known him, then?"

"Going on three months now. He interviewed and then I got to work figuring out how I wanted my bar set up. He had his ideas, and let me tell you, Missy, he don't like anything other than the best. He's got real nice taste. I'd've rather had a jukebox in the corner with some good ol' rock 'n' roll, but Crew insisted on a piano. I hate to admit it, but I like the piano. It's real nice."

"Does he pay you well?"

"Oh, yeah. I have no complaints there. He gives us more than any other place here would and he even offered me and the missus a honeymoon suite. Not right now, 'cause it's gonna be too busy for a while, but in the off season we getta get away from the kids and come be treated to the life of luxury. He works hard and plays even harder. Wow, do the ladies love him! I ain't seen him go a single day here without at least one hot girl trying to hang all over him. He doesn't seem like he minds the attention. Not a lick," Marlin finished with a knowing grin.

"I just bet," Haley answered, her eyes narrowing. She'd learned that about him, herself. That's why she wanted him to be her teacher so dang bad.

"Well, don't you worry, honey, he simply gives them a little kiss, then a night of lovin', then he slips right out of their grasp, and they never knew what hit 'em. They think he's the man of their dreams, but they wake up and it's all just been one big fantasy. Yet somehow they're grateful for even just a night. He's still available for ya. Maybe you can even make the rogue settle down," Marlin said with a chuckle.

"I don't want Crew for myself. I'm in love with another guy. I just want Crew to teach me his secrets — show me how to be one of those women men can't resist. But, you know what, I see a bar full of men who would probably be more than willing to teach me what I need to know," she said as she looked around the room.

The piano player was looking her way, and before she turned back to Marlin, the man gave her a wink. Oh yes, it was time to come out of her corner and fetch herself a teacher. Who said she couldn't mix business and *pleasure*?

"Sure, missy, sure. That's what they all say. If you think you can dance on a cliff without the wind pushing you over, then you just be my guest, but one night with a man like Crew and you'll forget all about this other guy you're trying to win."

"We'll just have to see about that," Haley said with confidence. "I think I'm going to request a song," she finished with a wink at Marlin. He just laughed and handed her a fresh drink.

As Haley stood up, feeling just a bit wobbly from too many of Marlin's drinks, she wished she knew how to sashay like a model, how to sway her hips provocatively. Oh, well. She'd have to do her best. With glinting eyes and a determined step, she approached the musician, and he wasn't taking his eyes off her.

Invisible? Not this time.

Chapter Six

Everything was running smoothly. Crew's staffers, all of whom he'd handpicked, were efficient, unobtrusive, and expert at anticipating a guest's needs. The customers were smiling and complimentary about his beautiful resort. On top of everything, they were spending — and spending plenty.

The kitchen staffers were working nonstop preparing stellar dishes, and room service orders were flooding in. This was a perfect grand opening. But somehow, Crew eventually found himself with a few minutes to spare.

He was drawn toward the bar, in part because he loved spending a few minutes with his head bartender. Marlin wasn't a pretty sight, but he was shrewd and knew his business. Each time Crew passed by, business was in full swing.

Stepping into the dimly lit, smoky room, he closed his eyes for the briefest of moments and enjoyed the sound of ice clinking in glasses while murmurs, chortles, and titters filled the room. Spirits were high, and the cash register was working overtime.

Business was good.

When Crew's potential buyer came in, he'd have nothing to fear in purchasing this establishment. It was a sure investment for anyone who was dedicated to continuing what Crew had started, because Crew didn't do anything by half measures.

Almost at the bar, he glanced back for the briefest of moments, started to go forward again and then whipped his head back around. He recognized that golden hair, even from a distance. The woman who'd propositioned him was cozying up real close to his pianist, and the guy didn't seem to mind one bit.

What should it matter to Crew? He didn't know her. If she had moved on to find the next man foolish enough to grant her request, then good for her. It meant she'd leave him alone.

If he felt that way, why was he suddenly changing direction and heading toward the happy couple? He was the owner of this establishment, that was why. He couldn't have her trying to prostitute herself to his staff. This place wasn't that kind of business.

As he approached, he saw her hand lift and settle on Sid's leg. His piano player just slid her a wink while his fingers continued to fly over the keys.

"That's lovely," she purred, her face inches from the guy's ear. Crew had heard enough.

"Ms. Sutherland," he said, his voice quiet but hard.

He had to give the woman credit, because her shoulders tensed in surprise for only the briefest of moments before she turned — slowly, quite slowly — to look at him.

"Hello, Mr. Storm. How nice to see you again." Her voice gave nothing away, but her big green eyes were pretty damned eloquent. The woman didn't need a teacher; her eyes alone had the power to seduce.

"I wasn't expecting to see you again — ever." His voice must have been more cold than he'd meant it to be, because his piano player stumbled on his notes before quickly recovering.

"I'm a determined woman, Mr. Storm. Now, if you don't mind, I was having a conversation with Sid. His music is breathtaking," she sighed before turning from Crew and giving him the brush-off. He had no idea that inside she was shaking terribly.

Crew didn't like her cavalier attitude. He was steaming, though he couldn't figure out exactly why. Though he'd wanted nothing to do with her proposition, he'd still had the woman on his mind all day, thinking of a million ways he could teach her, and now he found her in his resort looking for a man to fill her...bill. He wasn't appreciative, not in the least.

"I'd like to speak to you in private, Ms. Sutherland." It wasn't a request, but a command.

"I'm a little busy right now. Why don't we chat tomorrow?" With that, she dismissed him again.

Twice in a minute's time wasn't doing much for his ego.

"Why don't we do it now?" He took her arm and pulled her from the bench. The cowardly pianist continued playing as if Crew hadn't just manhandled his potential one-night stand. Crew would need to find a new player — he was disgusted with Sid.

Haley's eyes lit up. "If you insist," she said, slightly breathlessly, her head bent back so she could gaze at him.

His entire body tensed. Why was he attracted to this crazy woman? She was wearing a baggy T-shirt, another pair of loose Capri pants, and not a lick of makeup. There was nothing about her that screamed sex siren, and yet he found himself more than intrigued; what was she trying to hide with all those loose clothes?

As he started leading her from the bar and toward the lobby, the sound of her breathing shouldn't have scraped his nerves raw. She just wasn't his type in any way. Yet even the smell of peaches drifting from her hair was turning him on.

Maybe it had been too long since he'd spent the night with a woman. Those around him might have thought he was a lady killer, but not that many women had actually made it into his bedroom. He was choosy. Yes, he'd had the occasional one-night stand, but his reputation was a lot more rumor than reality.

He liked women, didn't like mistreating them, didn't like to use them for a night, only to walk away the next day. His father had taught him to be a better man than that. If the world wanted to believe he was a playboy, then let it. That only brought more people out of the woodwork to find out what he was about.

It was good for business, and it meant more money for him. Though his trust fund was more money than most people ever dreamed of having, it was only his if he passed his father's ridiculous test.

One problem: Crew just didn't care about the challenge anymore. He cared about what path in life he was on. If that meant the old man won, then so be it. Before starting on this resort, Crew hadn't realized it, but he really hadn't been able to look himself in the mirror without feeling shame at what he'd become. So much had changed, and he had to admit that he was grateful to his dad.

He passed the front counter, his staff barely glancing his way before going back to their work. Luckily, Haley had decided to keep her mouth shut while he led her to his private office.

He placed his hand on the small of her back and let her walk in ahead of him while he enjoyed the gentle sway of her hips. Once inside, he shut and locked the door. He didn't want interruptions. This woman just had to go away — he was too busy to deal with her request, or to watch her try to achieve her goals with other men.

Crew offered her a chair, then moved behind his desk, thinking it wiser for him to place a solid piece of furniture between the two of them. As she took her time sitting down, he noticed her eyes taking in everything around her. She was observant, well aware of her surroundings. This was a good quality to have, something to admire.

"I thought my room was nice, but this office is spectacular. I bet you a month's worth of groceries that the paintings are real," she said with a whistle.

Crew was about to make a snarky comment when her words hit him. "Your room?" He wanted clarification.

"Yes. I checked in tonight. I have to tell you, you know how to decorate. My room is fantabulous, and I haven't seen one tiny grain of sand inside this entire resort. That's impressive, considering we're right on the beach."

"Why did you check in?" he growled, coming right to the point.

"Because I won a terrific prize package back in Seattle and I get two spectacular weeks here. Are you saying I'm not welcome?" she asked a bit too innocently.

"I told you I wasn't willing to play your games, Haley, and yet you stalk me. Why not just leave?"

"I accepted your answer, Mr. Storm. Was I following you tonight? Did I seek you out? No, I did not. Just because you won't give me what I want doesn't mean that I will simply give up. I have a mission to complete, and there are plenty of men out there who can help me. Maybe I haven't seen any as charming as you — OK, *charming at times* — or with your knowledge of what it is that makes a woman sexy, but their advice and teaching should be enough to guide me to become the woman I wish to be. Besides, who in their right mind would give up two free weeks here?" she asked, looking at him as if he were certifiable.

Crew's vision was starting to blur. She spoke with such conviction that he had no doubt she would succeed in finding a suitable man. Shouldn't that be a good thing for him? She'd be out of sight, out of mind, not his problem. Unfortunately, she was his problem — for no reason he could figure, he actually cared what happened to her, and he shouldn't. Sheesh. He'd met this woman only this morning.

He had plans — goals — and he couldn't afford any distractions right now. His father would be here soon, and though Crew didn't care about his stupid trust fund any longer, he needed to prove to the man who had raised him that neither of them had wasted their time and effort.

"Who is this man you seek to attract? Why would you want someone who doesn't want you for who you are? I'm really just curious."

"Who he is doesn't matter. As for wanting me for who I am, that's more difficult. You wouldn't know anything about not being raised as a Storm, not having a privileged life from the moment you were born. You've always had everything, never had to struggle; you've never gone through troubles. You were born wealthy and beautiful. There is no way you could possibly have a clue what it's like for those of us on the other side," she spat out.

"I am *not* a snob." He was insulted she'd even think such a thing.

"Ha! I have always wondered if snobby people realize they're snobs. Do they go to bed at night thinking they're better than others? Do they snicker at people less fortunate than they are and go out of their way to make the poor saps' lives miserable? Or do they not know the pain and suffering they cause? As I look at the confusion in your eyes, I think I have my answer. Maybe some of them do and some of them don't. But I will tell you this: my years of school were a misery. The girls tormented me, called me names, made me feel horrible about myself. They sought joy through the pain they inflicted on me and others. Did it make them feel better about themselves, superior? Maybe. Maybe not. I really don't care. My revenge comes by having a good life now. I get revenge through my success. Part of that is by changing from being a girl who was so persecuted that I had to hide in the shadows just so they wouldn't notice me. I am done being afraid. I am done letting what other people think about me predict my actions. I am also done speaking to you. There is no way you will ever understand any of this."

Haley started to stand and Crew felt a moment's panic. What she said tore at him. Had he ever made someone feel like this? Either knowingly or unknowingly? If he had, it was unacceptable and to his eternal shame. He could never be OK with hurting another human for his own personal gain or pleasure.

"Please sit." His tone had calmed; his anger was deflated. How could he be angry with this woman, a woman who had so much hurt evident in her eyes? How could he possibly turn her away? Though he knew better than to accept her offer, he somehow couldn't chase away the desire to help.

And he knew he would regret this before the words came from his mouth.

"I will help you."

At first she just stared, but joy quickly overspread her face.

Crew shook his head gently. "Hold on before you get too excited. You have much more inside you than you realize, Haley. There is fire brewing in your veins, passion in your eyes, and what I'm sure is a pretty spectacular body beneath your ridiculously baggy clothes. I will help you to see yourself — not help you change who you are. There is nothing I see that needs changing."

He could tell by the shocked look on her face that she didn't believe him for a second. How cruel people must have been to her.

"I need to know a little bit about you," he continued. "Where you grew up. What your dreams are. What things you are attracted to. Before I can show you who you truly are, I need to know who you think you are."

Confusion covered her face. It was obvious she really had no idea of her own appeal. Her light green eyes peered at him through her befuddlement. Her soft blond hair cascaded down her back, most of it having worked loose from her sloppy bun. Even without makeup, she was a beauty. With it, she'd look like any one of the women who so confidently threw themselves at him. He preferred her the way she was now — well, maybe with tighter clothing.

"I am just me. You know my name's Haley Sutherland. I'm twenty-six; I went to school in

Washington state. I grew up with my grandparents, but they passed away several years ago. I have no idea who my dad is, and my mom died during childbirth. I have no other family members. My life has been boring up until now. I'm ready for excitement."

"Those are facts I could find out from the most basic of background searches. I will only agree to do this if you share with me — really share. I grew up with a younger sister who loved to talk, and talk often, so I know a little bit about what it is that makes women tick. I want to know your dreams, what excites you, what makes your heart pound. I need to know your fears, your darkest desires, the things you've thought about but never imagined telling anyone. I want to know *you*, Haley, not the image you show the world."

Crew watched as the shutters came down on her revealing eyes, closing him out. She was hiding something from him, and the competitive man he was wanted to know all her deepest secrets. He wanted to strip her bare, take her apart, and then help to build her back up. After all, that's what he did, wasn't it? He made things whole again. It couldn't be any more difficult than fixing a failing business.

"I don't want a mental makeover. I want you to teach me how to seduce a man. If I wanted to talk about my pathetic life, I'd see a psychiatrist."

Her snappy response showed him just how much she was holding back. Well, he would just have to call her bluff. If she walked, that was it. There was nothing he could do about it. He feared curiosity would eat him alive, but only for now. He'd eventually forget about her.

"Then we have nothing else to discuss. You can enjoy your stay in the resort, but I have more important things to do." Crew looked down at his desk, opened a drawer and pulled out a cigar, then snipped the end. He didn't indulge often, but when stress was at a peak, the smooth flavor of a good Cuban could ease his nerves.

Haley sat fuming as he waited for her to make a decision. Though he gave her no sign of what he was feeling, while he leaned back and propped his feet on the desk as if he didn't have a care in the world, his muscles were taut.

Crew played to win. There was no use in entering this game with her if she wasn't putting all her cards on the table. When the silence grew too long, he looked pointedly at his clock, and then at her face.

He almost feared seeing fire shooting from her eyes as she realized the bind she was in. For her to walk away when he'd agreed to her proposal would be mad on her part, but she clearly wanted to tell him to shove it.

Chapter Seven

"Fine. If you insist on trying to understand me, I'll tell you, but I'm tired right now and don't feel like talking," Haley responded. "It's been a long day."

She wanted to get up and kick his feet from the desk, then grab his stupid cigar and take a big puff for herself. But that would only end with her hacking up a lung, so she sat stiffly while she waited for whatever he had to say next.

"Good. Now that we have the practicalities out of the way, I can learn a little more about you."

The man just didn't listen. She didn't want to discuss anything about herself. She needed time to come up with a convincing story for him. There was no way she would tell him about the hell she'd gone through living with psychotic grandparents who had wished she were dead every single day of her life.

She'd buried the past, and to dig it back up again would do too much damage. It would destroy everything she'd worked at building over the last eight years. The moment they buried her bitter grandparents in the ground, she'd been freed. It had just taken her a long time to figure that out. To tell the truth, she was still learning.

"I don't think so, Haley. I believe you need time to regroup, time to come up with a clever story. I don't want to give you that time. I won't force you to tell me your entire life story, but I'd at least like to know something about you. Give me a small piece and I'll call it a night."

Haley scrambled to come up with something that wasn't too revealing, but the man seemed to have a built in radar for lies. It seemed that she had no choice but to part with a few honest details. In the end, it would all be worth it, because then she'd be one of those women she'd always admired, and she'd be free of the past.

"I plan on discovering an ancient culture that no one has ever discovered before. I don't care where, but I want to do an archeological dig. Ancient peoples fascinate me — how they worked so well together, how they survived such harsh conditions, and how they continued to procreate. I also have a fascination for old journals and the lives of people who lived before I was ever born." Maybe she'd revealed just a little more than she'd planned to, but when she spoke of her dream, she tended to get excited.

His eyebrows rose and the corners of his lips turned up. She had the sudden urge to smack the look off his face. The thought stunned her; she'd never felt desire to hit anyone, not ever, not even when those horrid kids at school had made her feel two inches tall.

"Do you have a journal of yours I can read?"

Now he was mocking her! She was done.

Haley stood quickly and began moving toward the door. There was nothing that made sitting here any longer worth it. She'd rather die a wallflower than be constantly humiliated.

"Haley, I was just kidding. You have to learn the difference between a joke and the intent to harm another person. I wasn't making fun of you," he said as he caught up to her at the door and gripped her arm.

A sensual fire shot down her arm from the touch of his firm grasp on her bare skin. Her legs felt weak and she was afraid to look up into his eyes. This wasn't what she wanted. She didn't want to feel an overwhelming sense of desire for a man she needed only as a teacher.

"Haley." The deep tone of his voice sent butterflies to her stomach. She needed to regroup. Subduing the strange feelings as forcefully as she could, Haley squared her shoulders and lifted her head, crooking the corner of her mouth and gazing at him with total disregard.

"You didn't hurt my feelings, Crew. I'm just done for the night. We can begin my transformation tomorrow." She was quite proud of her performance.

She knew as he gripped both her arms and pulled her close to him, though, that she hadn't fooled him. Still, she didn't reveal the effect he was having on her. That would be giving up too much, and she couldn't let the tables turn completely in his favor. She had pride, and she'd sunk as low as she was willing to allow herself.

"Mmm, Haley. The more I think about this, the more I am liking it. Can you feel the sparks?"

"What sparks?" she bluffed.

"You don't have to say it out loud. I can see the fire in your eyes, and I can feel your thighs quivering."

"Let go," she demanded, enraged that she was exposing so much of herself and her feelings to him when all she wanted was to run and hide. After all, that's what she was best at doing.

Crew held her for just a moment longer — just long enough to let her know he was stronger, could take what her eyes were offering him — then, he finally released his grip.

Haley wanted to bolt, run to her room, lock the door, and then slide down it and fold into herself. She wanted to do what she'd always done. But, wasn't this her seduction makeover? Wasn't it time for her to be that wanton woman she'd fashioned in her brain?

Before she could talk herself out of it, Haley reached up and grabbed his neck, pulling his head down to hers. She gloried in the shocked look in his eyes just before their lips connected.

"Lesson One: Take What You Want," she whispered. As his lips touched hers and his tongue quickly demanded entrance, Haley was nearly knocked flat. She was grateful there was a door behind her, because she had to lean against it as heat pooled deep within her.

72

Her mind blanked while her body flamed and their tongues danced back and forth between them. It was the steamiest kiss she'd ever shared — not that she'd shared many. Two, in fact, before this one.

When her brain started to completely short-circuit, she knew it was time to pull back. With extreme reluctance she broke the connection of their lips, with her tongue automatically emerging one last time to lick his flavor from her mouth.

"Well, that wasn't unpleasant," she said with a laugh that was far too breathy, and not as casual as she'd intended. If only she could clear the fog from her dazed brain, she could think enough to turn and leave the room. Eventually she got her feet to cooperate.

"Oh, no," Crew said with a huge smile as his hands shot around her and grabbed her from behind. "Lesson Two: When You Play with Fire, You Get Burned."

Before Haley could reply, he pulled her tightly against his body, the rock-hard evidence of his arousal pressing into her stomach as he leaned down and began kissing her again as if they'd never paused.

Taking a step back, he pressed her against his door, then moved his hands down the curve of her backside as he lifted her off her feet so he could press his straining manhood against her heat.

His mouth ravished hers, showing no mercy as he stole the air right from her lungs, and sizzled her skin. She forgot why she needed to stay in control, forgot everything as he continued taking her deeper and deeper into the throes of passion.

Had she known years earlier how explosive a kiss could be, she wouldn't have remained a virgin, wouldn't have let her grandparents' constant voice in her head keep her from enjoying something so amazing.

For the first time ever, she was alive, wanting only to sink further and further into sensation, to feel the passion he was so easily igniting. She pressed against him, her hands fisting in his hair as she silently begged him to continue —never, ever to stop filling her with the magical emotions she was losing herself in.

When a low growl rumbled deep in his chest, a feeling of power surged through Haley at her beginner's luck. She'd turned this man into an animal bent only on fulfilling his needs. She'd brought this handsome, powerful playboy to a state of no return.

When his mouth softened on hers, she wanted to scream out in passion. When he pulled back, sliding his tongue across her bottom lip before pulling all the way back and setting her on her feet, she felt disoriented, not even sure if she *could* stand.

"Do you still think there are no sparks, Haley?" he asked, his voice drifting over her as his breath warmed her neck. She thought she felt the barest of kisses, but then he pulled back so she was looking into his eyes.

Haley didn't know how to respond. Should she be flippant? Laugh it off? Or should she just run away until she figured it out?

No.

"I've had better," she finally managed to reply, her voice not particularly thick and uneven. He narrowed his eyes before he leaned into her for the briefest of moments, showing her again what their kisses had done to him — how hard he was.

"I somehow don't think so," he answered confidently. "Go get some rest. You will need it," were his last words before he grabbed her hand and pulled her away from the door so he could open it. "Would you like me to escort you upstairs?"

The knowing tone of his voice had her back straightening. "I'm capable of reaching it safely in your well-secured resort," she said, acting casually as she stepped through the door. "Sweet dreams," she threw over her shoulder as her gaze slid down his body and landed pointedly on his bulging pants.

The curse word that followed her down the hall lifted her spirits.

Power.

She now knew what it was like to feel power in the arms of a man. As Haley made her way dreamily up the elevator and let herself into her suite, she didn't even realize she hadn't once thought about Walker, the man she...wanted.

Chapter Eight
Two months earlier

Joseph and George pulled up to the Storm Corporate offices and looked at each other. The building was sleek and modern, not overly large, but charming and well-built; it fit in nicely with the busy business district.

Large glass panels reflected the sun, announcing its presence among the other structures around it. The brothers made their way inside and nodded with appreciation at the appealingly cut gray marble. The silver and black color scheme and modern decor of the building's interior welcomed visitors but filled them with awe at the same time.

"It seems our brother has true Anderson blood running through his veins. He has good taste."

"He certainly does. Now remember, we don't want to overwhelm him," Joseph reminded George.

"I think he's going to be quite shocked when he faces us, Joseph. There's no getting past the good looks that run in our blood," George joked.

"Well, when you're right, you are right," Joseph said with a wink.

They approached the front desk, where a pretty young secretary looked up with a professional smile before her expression froze and she did a double take. It was almost comical to see her eyes flash between George and Joseph's faces.

"Um...how...how can I help you?" she stuttered as she tried to gather her wits.

"We're here to see Richard Storm."

"Do you...um...have an appointment?"

"No, darling, we don't, but I think he'll want to meet with us," Joseph said as he leaned forward and gave her his most appealing smile. He was a master negotiator, after all.

"He doesn't normally see people without an appointment," she answered, still a bit shell-shocked.

"I think he'll make an exception. Just let him know it's relatives of his," George told her with a wink.

The woman fumbled for the phone and pressed a button. She leaned away, speaking quietly, but the two men were both sure she was saying something like *Richard's look-alikes are here.* They'd had a few hours to process the possibility of having a brother. The rest of the world was in for a big shock.

"His executive secretary said to come on up. He's on the twelfth floor. She'll see you there," the woman said and handed them both an elevator pass.

After thanking her, the two headed straight but not swiftly to the elevator. Neither of them would admit to the nervous butterflies dancing around in their stomachs, but they pressed the button for the twelfth floor in silence and just stared at the metal doors.

They got the same reaction from the woman behind another efficient modern desk when they introduced themselves as Joseph and George Anderson.

"What is your business with Mr. Storm?" She was keeping it together a bit more than the first woman, but they could see that she couldn't stop looking at them both with a wary and assessing eye.

"It's private family business, ma'am," George calmly stated.

After a moment on the phone, she hung up and faced them. "Follow me, please." Neither of them was surprised. They weren't used to being denied anything they wanted, so they'd have been more shocked had they not gotten in.

When the secretary knocked on a door, a voice called out telling them to enter. The man had his back to them as he looked out his window at the picturesque view of the Sound. Both Joseph and George had spent a lot of their own time in a similar position in front of their office windows.

The woman left the room, though they could see her reluctance and the curiosity in her eyes as she casually departed. They noticed that she left the door open. Joseph also noticed the guard not far away, prepared to rush forward in an instant if he was needed.

When Richard Storm turned around with an indulgent smile on his face as if he were about to appease a couple of batty old men, it didn't take long for his jaw to slacken as he stared at the two strangers.

"Hello Richard. This is my brother, George, and I'm Joseph. We believe we have a lot to talk about," said Joseph as he approached the man he had no doubt was his brother.

After a moment's pause, Richard pulled himself together and held out a hand. "Have we met before?"

"No. Trust me, we'd all remember," George cut in as he took the man's hand next. "We believe we're related, though." There was no need to beat around the bush. They'd already lost sixty-plus years.

"I can see why you'd think so. How do you know about me? I have been careful over the years to stay out of the media. Who are you?" As if he were unable to stand anymore, he moved to a seating area in the corner of his spacious office and sank down into a chair.

The Anderson brothers joined Richard. "Let me explain…" George said.

Joseph pulled out the documents they'd brought and George told Richard what they'd put together that afternoon, with Joseph filling in any gaps. Richard said nothing at all. After half an hour, the three men sat there just staring at each other.

79

"This can't be. My parents…they were good people," Richard finally choked out as he looked at the compelling evidence before him.

"We can always get blood tests," Joseph said, firmly but gently. "I think that would be a good idea, but it's like looking in a mirror to be staring at you. You can see the picture of our father here. We take most after him."

"My father was Thomas Storm no matter what a blood test says," Richard said automatically.

"Yes, he raised you and obviously loved you, but I believe you are our brother. I believe our mother and father never knew you existed." Joseph said the words in the kindest way he could, but Richard had to know the truth. They couldn't possibly lose any more time.

"I just don't understand. If this is true, maybe your parents didn't want three children. Maybe they'd made a deal with my parents…" The man was reaching for straws, not wanting to believe his parent would be capable of kidnapping.

"That is something we will never know, Richard, and it's something we don't have to know. Your parents obviously loved you, as ours loved us. We just want you to be a part of our lives if you're our brother. Family is very important to us," George said as he leaned forward.

"I don't know what to say. I need some time. I will send for blood tests right away, though. I have never been a man to hide from the truth, and if you are my brothers, I would very much like to know about you and your families."

"That goes the same for us, Brother. I don't know what made you decide to move back to Seattle, but we are grateful it happened," George said with a big smile.

The men chatted for a few minutes more before Joseph and George left.

They took the blood tests the next day and, with the help of their wealth and influence, had their answer by that afternoon. Richard Storm was indeed their brother, with identical DNA. That didn't answer the question of how he'd been separated from them at birth, whether Richard's adoptive parents had taken him, or whether their biological parents had given him up, but Joseph and George knew their parents — knew they would never part with one of their own.

They didn't need to repeat that to Richard, however. The past couldn't be changed, and all they could do from this moment on was to get to know one another, become the family they should have been all along. It might be a long journey, but family bonds were hard to break, and determination was in the Anderson blood.

The hearts of all three men raced as they considered the prospect of learning about each other and their thriving families.

Chapter Nine

Crew sat back and finished his cigar while he waited for his body to return to normal. Haley Sutherland might have thought she needed training on how to become the perfect seductress, but if the way she'd kissed was any indication, she was miles ahead of any woman he could think of off the top of his head.

Damn, his body was on fire, and he didn't see it returning to a functioning state any time soon. She'd set his world spinning, and he suspected it wasn't going to stop until he taught her a few horizontal lessons.

The smile spreading across his lips caused faint crow's-feet to crinkle at the corners of his eyes. He would bet his resort that she was fire beneath the sheets. All of that repressed energy would explode as he sank deep within her heat.

He groaned. Those thoughts hadn't helped at all — his erection was now pulsing painfully in his pants. He desperately needed something, anything as a distraction.

As if on cue, his telephone rang and he picked up without thinking.

"Crew Storm."

"I'm heading down there soon, and I have company."

"Dad?" The brisk excitement in his father's tone surprised him. He couldn't remember hearing him so elated, not in years, at least.

"Of course, it's your father. Who else?" he asked sourly.

"Sorry. What's going on?"

"You remember when I called you a couple of months ago about those two men stopping by my office?"

"Vaguely. You said they might be relatives of ours or something." Crew had been tied up in last-minute preparations for the resort. He could barely remember the conversation.

"Well, they *are* related. That's all I'm going to say until we get there. I want you to see for yourself. I will tell you that I've gotten to know them and they are good men — very good men. I think you will like them. I think they may even rival us in large families," he said with a sly chuckle.

"Sounds good, Father. It's nice for you to find some long-lost relatives. But I thought your adoption records were sealed. Are you sure you want to open all of that up?"

"I'm absolutely sure, son," he answered.

"That's good." Crew didn't know what else to say.

"How did your grand opening go? I'm looking forward to seeing what you've achieved."

"It went even better than I'd hoped. A lot has changed since you were here six months ago. I will miss this place…" he sighed as he looked around his office. The more he thought about it, the more he didn't want to let her go. Still, he was sure his attachment would fade as the excitement of new beginnings wore off.

"You don't have to, Crew. I know I told you that was the deal — that you all make a profit selling the businesses — but I think you've learned what I wanted you to. I'm very proud of you. In the end you have to choose if you want to settle in one place, or if you've found your passion and want to do it again and again with new projects."

The sudden choking in his father's voice came through the telephone line loud and clear. Crew didn't know what to say. In all his life, he'd never heard his father cry. It just didn't happen.

Crew quickly changed the subject. "Give me the dates you're coming down so I can make sure to have our best rooms available for you."

"We'll need three rooms, and any will do. The point is to see you, not to vacation," Richard said, then he promised to give his son a heads up when he knew a more exact time of his arrival.

"Three rooms? I'll have to check, but I save a block for emergencies, so I think we'll be fine." He paused for a moment. It needed to be said, but it was hard for him to get the words to come out. "Dad, you did a good thing — a really good thing."

Crew wasn't going to elaborate. His father had a big enough head already. When Richard was silent for several seconds, Crew thought they might have lost the connection. Then, he realized that his dad was just trying to regain his composure.

"Thank you, Crew. Now, enough business talk. Have you managed to find a woman yet?"

Classic. The statement made Crew laugh into the phone receiver. "No, father. I'm not looking for love. One step at a time."

"You know, you aren't getting any younger, boy. You'll be thirty-five on your next birthday. It's time to settle down and keep the family name alive. A good woman will add years to your life."

Something about the sadness of his tone alerted Crew that something was wrong, but he couldn't figure out what it might be. It was most likely just his imagination, anyway. His father was as strong and vibrant as ever. If anything were worrying him, he would be sure to tell his children, despite their reprehensible behavior before Richard finally laid down the law.

"I'm not quite ready, Dad, but I'll let you know when I find the one. As for kids, I don't see that happening. I'm not the 'dad type,'" he said, taking a large puff from his cigar and blowing the air out.

"That's utter nonsense, boy!" his father snapped, sounding much more like himself.

The tense muscles in Crew's neck relaxed. One worry down. And at least he wasn't thinking about bedding Haley Sutherland. Unfortunately, if it wasn't one kind of stress, it was another. His arousal had disappeared, and his father seemed just fine, but once again, he had his father on his back, pushing him to get married and settle down. It seemed there would be no relaxation for him today.

"Dad…" he warned.

"I'm getting to be an old man, Crew, and I demand to have some grandchildren before the good Lord decides to take me from this earth. I don't see what's so wrong with that request. Why, most people my age have at least ten grandchildren, but oh no, not me. My kids don't think about raising the next generation. They don't think about bringing me some happiness in my declining years…" Richard continued to rant for several long minutes, making Crew set down the phone and rush to the liquor cabinet, where he poured himself a shot of scotch. He needed something warm and soothing in his bloodstream. He knew this stupid speech by heart — he'd been hearing it for years, and he knew he wouldn't miss a thing.

When Crew picked the phone back up, his father was nearing the end of his whine. "…and that's why you need to settle down!"

"You'd better not be doing any more scheming. I still haven't forgiven you for that time Sue Ellen and I managed to get locked in the boathouse overnight when I was twenty-four," Crew reminded his father.

"I don't know what you're talking about. I wasn't the one who locked you in, if that's what you're implying. But, at the age of twenty-four, you were more than ready to be married. Heck, by now, you should have at least three kids. I wouldn't mind each of you having a dozen of the little ankle-biters."

"I get it, Dad. You want grandkids. Talk to Lance. He's more likely to give them to you than the rest of us."

Crew felt a slight pang at selling out his brother, but Lance was more the father type, if there were such a thing. Their dad, with his incredible dedication, had given his children a great example of what a father should be, and it wasn't that Crew didn't want kids; it was just something he didn't anticipate in the foreseeable future. Time to cut this call short.

"Hey, Dad. I'm sorry, but I'm getting a call on the other line," he told him, grateful for the flashing red light. He wouldn't tell an outright lie, but he'd suffered through his father's guilt trip long enough; reports of zombies in the spa pool might have sounded good in comparison.

"Fine, fine. But you'll have no choice but to listen when I show up down there," Richard said.

"Yes, you can give me the talk about family obligation again, and again, very soon," Crew told him. His tone was genial, and he hoped his remark wouldn't set his dad off. Luckily, it didn't, and he was able to say goodbye.

Crew missed the incoming call, but wasn't too worried about it. After hanging up the phone, he looked at the clock and found to his surprise that it was nearing midnight. Time really flew when you weren't having fun. Since he had an early-morning meeting, he decided to call it a night.

Switching his phone over to the emergency desk, Crew locked up the office and headed to his private suite.

Had he known he was going to spend the night sweating in bed with erotic dreams starring Haley, he'd have stayed up and caught up on work instead.

Chapter Ten

Crew woke up in a foul mood. He'd tossed and turned most of the night, finally giving up on sleep at five in the morning, stumbling from his bed and heading straight to the shower.

He would have just guffawed had a fortune-teller laid out his tarot cards and said: "I see in your future a crazy blond woman wearing shapeless clothes. She will approach you with an indecent proposal, and you'll be unable to do anything but think about her."

Both awake and asleep.

After washing the sweat from his body, Crew planned his day. There was no time like the present, he decided, to begin his damnable lessons. In order for Haley to become the seductress she wanted to be, she needed first to feel like a beautiful woman.

This was something Crew knew how to do. He loved the courting game, though it had been a while.

A man who didn't spoil his woman or treat her like his most valuable treasure wasn't worthy of her love. And, hey, it could be fun.

Romance didn't always mean large gestures. Often it was the small things that mattered most. A note telling her how beautiful she was, a single rose laid upon her pillow at night, a chocolate sitting next to her coffee cup. Small things to let her know she was always on his mind.

Crew was often confused by his fellow men. He didn't see how guys were so blind to what women wanted and needed. Haley wanted to make men flock to her, but it would help her to find out — and she was about to — why women flocked to him, and how he chose a woman.

Once she knew how incredibly intoxicating she was, she'd be the type of girl he would have approached a week ago. Her only flaw was her lack of confidence. She didn't realize it, but the only thing he was teaching her was how to love herself — everything else would easily fall into place for her after that.

First on his list of to-dos was to order a large bouquet of pink and purple stargazer lilies, making sure the greenery matched the color of her eyes and the flowers themselves were fragrant enough that each time she entered the room, their smell would tease and delight her senses.

He also ordered breakfast to be delivered, heading to the kitchen himself to ensure that no mistakes were made. He'd yet to find a woman who couldn't be seduced by silky chocolate and vibrant flowers. The longer she was with him, the more expensive the gifts, but in the beginning, subtlety was best.

Sliding the delicate chocolate truffles onto her plate and attaching a note, Crew smiled and waited for her call. It didn't take long — about twenty minutes, in fact.

"Crew?" her sleepy voice drifted through the phone line, to his ear.

"Speaking," he said softly as he made his way toward her room.

"You have an impressive way of wangling a breakfast invitation," she said, her voice soft and husky from sleep.

"I do what I can," he replied as he neared her door.

"The flowers are beautiful, and this chocolate is the best I've ever had," she mumbled around the sweet concoction in her mouth. As Crew pictured filling her mouth with much more than chocolate, his groin tightened. Man, he wanted her sweet, full lips around his shaft – hell, all over his body, but especially his shaft!

"Are you going to invite me in?" he practically whispered. To himself, he said: *Down, boy!*

"Well…you did have breakfast for two sent up. I hate to see such a good meal wasted…"

"Invite me in, Haley. This is Lesson Three," he said, his voice purposely low and seductive. Satisfaction filled him at the hitch in her voice.

"I need time to get dressed."

"Then our breakfast will get cold. You look fine, I'm sure," he said with a hint of impatience. He really wanted to know what she slept in. Was it nothing at all? The sudden thought had his blood racing.

"Fine. Come on up," she conceded.

"I'm already here. Open the door." Crew hung up and waited. He had the master key in his pocket, but he wouldn't use it. She needed to have the confidence in herself to let him through her door.

The door opened just a crack and Crew first saw big green eyes peering out at him. He said nothing, just raised his eyebrows as he waited for her to open the door all the way.

He wanted to push his way through, take her in his arms, and taste the chocolate on her tongue, but he was supposed to be teaching *her*. This wasn't about his own needs, though he promised himself they would get met.

By the time he was finished with Haley Sutherland, she'd never think again about this other man she'd been so desperate to capture. Of course, it wasn't as if Crew wanted to find himself captured either. He just needed a few nips of her perfect skin, a few cries of passion from her slender throat, and a few whimpers and gasps for air as she fell apart in his arms.

"Are you going to let me in, Haley, or just stand behind the door gaping at me?" he asked with a smile.

She narrowed her eyes, then rolled them as she gave him enough room to step through. Crew waited patiently for the door to shut firmly behind him before he made eye contact.

He was grateful for his decision, because when he turned and saw her, his jaw nearly dropped. She was wearing nothing but a pair of men's flannel boxers and a tight tank top, displaying *exactly* what she'd been hiding beneath those baggy clothes.

To make matters worse, the white cotton tank was just the slightest bit too thin, showing him the shadow of her dark nipples beneath the soft fabric. His throat went dry and he took an involuntary step toward her.

As if she knew exactly what he was thinking, she turned quickly and raced toward the bathroom, calling out that she'd be right out. Damn! She was most likely covering up all that beautiful skin.

Lesson Four was coming real quick, because if she wanted to seduce a man, she was certainly more than qualified to do it.

Crew sat at the table, pouring himself a cup of hot coffee and releasing a deep breath while he sat back in his chair and waited. It didn't take her long, but when she returned, he found that he'd predicted correctly: she was wearing too many clothes.

"You should have stayed in your pajamas," he said, disappointed by the oversized knit shirt she'd thrown on. At least her slender legs were still on display.

"I was cold," she lied.

"No you weren't, Haley. That shirt hid nothing, and if you had been cold, I would have known about it," he smirked.

Her cheeks flamed; she picked up a croissant and began nibbling on its corner in hopes of hiding her embarrassment.

"Thank you for the lilies — they're my favorite, but you really don't need to do that. I asked you to teach me how to be the one to seduce a man. There's absolutely no need for *you* to try to seduce *me*," she said crisply as she poured tea into a cup and added a little lemon and sugar.

Crew waited until he had her full attention before he spoke, making sure to capture her eyes with his gaze. He wanted her to have no doubt where this was going.

"I don't do anything by half measures, Haley. I agreed to your ridiculous request, but I'm going to be the one in charge here. If you are to become anything like the kind of woman you're asking me to make you, then we do it my way — without any complaints. Today's lesson: you must realize your own appeal. A woman who *feels* sexy *is* sexy. You don't have to be a model — you can be too thin or too large — and you don't have to be the perfect height or have the perfect curves. You just have to know how to use what you've got, and display it in the best possible light."

Haley looked down as if making a catalog of her best points. Then she shook her head and frowned.

"What are my assets, then?"

That she honestly didn't know made Crew's breath catch in his throat. Man, was he turned on. He didn't know if he'd make it through this "lesson." Her innocence was…exciting.

Instead of answering her, Crew stood up from the table. He'd lost all his appetite…for food, that was. She tensed as he circled around her and kneeled behind her low-back chair. But, to her credit, she didn't pull away when he rested his hands on her shoulders.

"First off, your hair. It's stunning. The color is golden, and the strands are long and soft." As he spoke, his fingers glided through her hair. Even after a night's sleep, it was sleek and smooth to the touch.

"Then there are your eyes — the soft green shines with vibrancy and life when you aren't looking down. Fire flashes in them when you're determined or irritated. Passion pours out of them when you're turned on." His hand moved to her cheekbones as he spoke, his body pressing against the back of the chair. He didn't want her to look at him, just feel his hands caressing her, and let his words cascade through her so she could focus wholly on herself.

"Don't forget your neck; its taut, creamy skin with your pulse beating just below the surface can drive a man wild," he whispered in her ear as he leaned forward and circled his hands around her throat, his fingers gentle as he caressed her.

Her pulse was speeding up, making his own race. He moved to the side of the chair so he could stroke her cheek and run his lips across her smooth skin. Her responses to him were fueling his desire, but he refused to let himself get out of control. This was about teaching her to embrace her sexuality, not about seducing her, even if it killed him.

"Then, of course, we start to reach the perfection of your breasts. When you don't hide them, they can drop a man to his knees. They're firm and high and just the right fit for a man's large hands," he groaned as his hands moved downward and grazed over the outside of her shirt, shaping her luscious curves with his palms.

Her nipples hardened beneath his touch; her body went limp in the chair and her head fell backward. Crew knew he could lift her in his arms and take her to the bed — make her his right now. With a will he didn't know he had, he forced himself to continue his demonstration.

"Your hips are curved and perfect, making a man want to grip them tightly in his hands while he pulls you against his body and fits himself right at the edge of glory. I could take you right now and feel a deep, satisfying pleasure from my head to my toes," he said as he rubbed his hands down her hips before coming around the front of her chair.

He knelt before her, then took her hips again and pulled her forward, her legs spreading around his thighs, aligning her heat perfectly with his excruciatingly hard manhood.

Gripping her backside, he squeezed her firm, yet soft tush as her eyes opened the tiniest fraction of an inch and she looked at him with fire leaping from those beautiful green depths of hers.

"I won't continue telling you about the most appealing pieces of you, because if I do, this lesson will end with me taking you hard and fast, and we're not there yet, Haley. But, I want you to go into the bathroom, strip naked and run your hands over your body. I want you to close your eyes as you touch yourself, feel what I'm feeling. I want you to feel what makes you so sexy — feel what will make a man crawl over hot coals to touch."

Crew pulled her against him for just one moment — just a brief second, it seemed — to try to alleviate the pain throbbing in his groin. Then he moved her back and lifted her hands, placing them both on her chest, causing her eyes to snap open, arousal clouding her vision.

"Go do it, Haley. Go complete your lesson," he groaned as she automatically flexed her fingers, making the muscle in his jaw jump from the amount of restraint he was exerting over himself.

In a daze, Haley stood up, her legs shaky. Without a word, she turned and went toward the bathroom. He didn't know whether she'd do what he asked or not right at this moment, but he knew it would sink in and she'd eventually follow through.

He sat back down, seriously thinking about grabbing a glass of the ice water on the table and dumping it down his ridiculously tight trousers. When he heard a soft groan from the bathroom as the shower started, he nearly lost it.

This lesson was over. Crew stood up and grabbed a sweatshirt he saw hanging over a chair. Draping it across his arm, he hid the enormous erection he was sporting and practically sprinted from her room.

Only one employee tried to speak to him as he made a beeline to his suite. He ignored the woman and dashed into his room. He locked his door behind him and barely paused before heading straight to the shower, scattering his clothes along the way. This adventure with Haley wasn't going to be good for his body — not one little bit.

Chapter Eleven

For the next five days, Crew tested the very limits of what he could handle. He didn't know whether he was a glutton for punishment or if he was determined to walk around with certain body parts south of the equator forever swollen. Haley was an eager learner, which made everything, er…harder. If she had been impatient or snooty, this would have been so much easier on him.

He could write her off — say he'd tried and then get her out of his head. But the light of excitement shining in her eyes each time he showed her something new was intoxicating for him. The moment was approaching when he would take her to the furthest reaches she could imagine.

That was a lesson that must be taught — personally. Though she wouldn't admit to him how many sexual partners she'd been with, he knew it couldn't be many. She was too shy, too unaware of her own body to have slept with more than a few men. Heck, he wouldn't be surprised if she'd been with only one or two.

Well, by the time he was done teaching her, she'd be a regular siren in bed. Unfortunately, the thought of her using these skills, the skills *he'd* taught her, with another man sparked a nasty little twinge in his gut. But he wasn't going to dwell on that now

As he walked toward her door, he was determined to keep his hands to himself. The touching had been a part of teaching her to appreciate herself, but that wasn't on the syllabus for today. Today was Lesson Ten — or was it Twelve? — he couldn't remember. Anyway, they were going shopping. The loose clothing had to go. She was a stunner, and she needed to show that off.

He'd have her fitted for a body-hugging gown, pick out a few outfits, and then take her out for a romantic dinner and dancing. Every man in the room would be jealous and every woman would want to be Haley Sutherland. If she didn't feel alive at the end of the day, he'd be earning a failing grade.

Bright-eyed and smiling, he almost bounced from his office, and was immediately stopped by his head manager, who was able to suppress his surprise at the boss's bizarre cheeriness and was not to be deflected from a discussion of some documents. Typical. But business always came before pleasure, or it should.

*****

Looking out at the ocean waves crashing against the shores of the island had Haley excited to get away from the resort for a while. She'd heavily pursued Crew and been persistent in persuading him to be her teacher, but she felt as if she couldn't breathe while in his presence. The man was so overwhelming — and what was worse, she wanted his touch, wanted more of him.

She enjoyed when he touched her – wanted more of it. She was trying to remember that she'd *hired* him — was it still hiring him if he wouldn't accept pay? — oh, well, that didn't matter. It was just a technicality.

The point was that she had hired him so she could catch her man, not so she could be caught by her teacher. But she had to remind herself of that every minute she spent with him. And that was a lot of minutes.

How *did* he manage to run his resort so successfully when he was constantly at her side? He had gathered an amazingly efficient staff, and he did work hard in the morning. And he kept checking in with his employees when they were in and out of the resort during the rest of the business day.

It was the nights that were the hardest. When he held out a chair for her and gently pushed her in, his fingers skimmed over her neck and her skin tingled for long minutes afterward. When the palm of his hand rested on the small of her back or when he whispered evocative words in her ear, oh, her resistance was low. She'd never intended to sleep with him, but her will was breaking.

What would it be like to have a man's hands caress her body, to have his mouth travel down the side of her neck and then capture her swollen nipple, wetting it with his tongue? It seemed that was all she thought about lately.

Before, when she pictured a man lying with her, the images hadn't been nearly as vivid and the face hadn't belonged to Crew Storm. For that matter, the man had always been faceless. She'd never really thought about that fact. It certainly hadn't been the face of Walker, the man she'd believed she wanted so very badly.

Scratch that. She did want him, she did! This was just a matter of her spending too much time with Crew. Of *course* the man was going to get inside her head.

Crew was dangerously masculine — sinfully, in fact. He was everything she should avoid, but he was her teacher, so how could she stay away? She smiled at the thought. It wasn't her fault if she was just following through on her plan, right? If something *did* happen between the two of them, it was just Crew teaching her, wasn't it?

If only she didn't have the voice of her grandparents still in her head, making her feel so guilty about her thoughts. She was planning on having sex, so what did it matter if it was with her teacher or the man she intended to pursue? Nothing seemed to make sense anymore.

Well, she wouldn't be a fool. She wouldn't do something rash like fall for him. She was just suffering from a minor case of lust; that was all. It was perfectly normal — nothing to get too worked up about.

Her spirits reviving, Haley turned from the magnificent ocean view off her balcony and headed into the bathroom, shedding the robe that had been a gift from Crew. The soft pink silk slid over her skin, making her feel feminine and sexy.

It was silly, really, how just a piece of material — even expensive material — could change how you felt about yourself. When she tied the soft sash around her waist and looked in the mirror, she felt…sensual.

It didn't take her long to shower and then to pad naked out to her bedroom, where she pulled open the closet doors and looked inside with disgust. Never before had she given much thought to what she wore, but as she looked at her bland clothing, all in shades of beige, white and dull pastels, she wished for something different.

After wearing the ultrafeminine nightie and robe, she wanted something nice for the daytime, too. Staring hopelessly into her closet, she knew she couldn't wave a magic wand and suddenly change what was in there, so she needed just to close her eyes and take the first thing she touched.

But a sudden inspiration hit her. Crew had made her appreciate her legs as he'd run his hands up them, commenting on what nice muscle tone she had. So Haley grabbed one of her long skirts and a pair of scissors, along with the small sewing kit in the bathroom. Slipping her robe back on, she laid the skirt out on the bed and began to rip out stitches to make a long slit up one side, to stop at the top of her thigh. With a wide grin, she took the skirt to the ironing board provided in her suite.

She was quick to secure the hems with an invisible stitch, and when she slipped into the skirt and took a step, she felt daring and bold. If a strong wind blew, her legs would be on display. For the very first time, she felt the desire to wear something so sexy. Turning to look in the mirror, she wiggled her hips, feeling slightly attractive even with her all-too-white thighs so blatantly revealed. At least she'd just shaved, she thought, as she made her leg shimmy, loving the effect from the impromptu slit in the soft material.

Her next dilemma was a shirt. Only her sleep shirts were even *sort of* fitted, so she'd have to get creative again.

She took one of her button-up blouses and cut off the sleeves, being careful not to make it looked hacked apart, and she rolled the cut edges and threw in another quick hem job. Then, putting the blouse on, she left the bottom five buttons undone and pulled the corners forward, tying a loose knot so the shirt rested just above the waistline of her skirt. About an inch of skin showed when she moved. Better and better.

So why not be even more daring? Haley unbuttoned the top three buttons, then looked in the mirror, blushing slightly at what she saw. If Crew wasn't knocked for a loop, she'd be crushed. The way the skirt rode low on her hips and the blouse was tied at her waist made her look as if she had an hourglass figure.

"Not too bad," she murmured as she turned to go back into the bathroom and tie her hair up into a somewhat sexy bun with a small braid running through it, and wisps of hair flying around her face. Yes, Crew had told her that he loved the way her hair cascaded halfway down her back, but it was a warm day and she didn't want to be uncomfortable. She did wear it down in the evenings, though it drove her a little bit mad when it kept falling in her face.

Deciding she was as ready for the day as she'd ever be, she glanced at the clock; the little hand on the eleven surprised her. She gathered up money, sliding it into her small handbag, then grabbed her sunglasses and made it to the door.

It didn't take her long to reach the lobby, and she thought she might actually make her escape when Crew's rich baritone voice caught her at the door. She'd planned on seeing him after her shopping, hopefully getting a bit of color in her cheeks, and time to think about how far she was willing to go with him in his lessons.

But it looked as if sneaking away from him in his own resort was easier said than done.

"We may not need to have shopping lessons, after all."

Hesitating for only a moment before she turned with a false smile, Haley replied without thinking: "I'm on my way out now to look for clothes." She shouldn't have told him her plans

"Good. I'm ready to leave."

"I wasn't inviting you this time. Last I knew, men despised shopping," she said with an air of indifference, trying to suggest that she wasn't bothered whether he came along or not. She didn't want him to know how much he was getting under her skin.

She needed him for a while longer — she knew that — so she couldn't let on that she was actually attracted to him. Men like Crew Storm liked to reel women in, and then cast them back out to sea as soon as they made their catch.

As long as he thought he was still on the hunt, he'd continue helping her. Once he knew how infatuated she was becoming, how easily she was taking the bait, he'd head for the hills in horror.

Propping her hand on her hip, she took a casual stand. *Resist! Resist*! she told herself.

"I love to shop. And that happens to be our lesson plan today," he said as he grabbed her arm and then entwined their fingers. Dang it!

"Sorry, Crew, but today's mission is solo. I'll catch up with you later tonight. You can teach me how to make eyes at cute guys." She laughed as she tried to pull her hand from his.

"Tough. I want to be with you this afternoon. Besides, I know what men like to see on a woman, and isn't that why you 'hired' me — to teach you how to be a sex goddess?"

He had her there.

She hadn't even realized it, but while he'd been cajoling her, he'd also been moving her outside, and soon he was holding open the passenger door of his car.

"Where do you plan on taking me?" she asked, submitting to the inevitable. Her day to herself was over.

"Shopping, of course," he replied. "I said that before."

"That's hardly an answer, but *fine*. If you insist on taking me, then you're buying." She figured that would make him reconsider.

Wrong.

He grinned as he helped her get in. "It will be my pleasure," he said with a bow before jogging to the other side of the car and getting in.

When they arrived at the airstrip a few minutes later, she turned with suspicion. He said nothing as he jumped from the car, then came around to her side. It wasn't until they were heading toward the helicopter that she realized he planned to take her up in the air in that death trap.

"No way!" she yelled and began to back away.

"Oh, you really need to live a little," he said, chuckling as he lifted her into his arms and carried her the rest of the way, unceremoniously plopping her into the seat.

Before Haley could protest any further, he had her strapped in, and soon the miserable, claustrophobic contraption was lifting off into the air. She just closed her eyes and prayed they wouldn't end up as food for the Pacific Ocean fishes.

Chapter Twelve

Haley's arrival at Santa Catalina Island had been by ferry — a nice, safe way to travel across an ocean, she insisted to herself. And she had endured the thirty-seven-hour train trip from Seattle to Long Beach, not tempted by any airlines that promised to get her from Point A to Point B in less than three hours. She had vowed never, ever to fly in a helicopter, never wanting to have that feeling of not being in control. On the ground, if you fell, you didn't have far to go, but way up in the sky... Splat!

She wasn't as terrified of huge airliners as she was by tiny helicopters, which had a far higher fail rate than jets, but still, she would only fly if it were a life and death matter. Going shopping on the mainland was certainly not an emergency. It could, however, end up being a death matter if the pilot screwed up in even the smallest way.

A shudder raced through her as she listened to the rotors spin. Luckily, the ride didn't take long. She didn't care what Crew would attempt to say — she wouldn't even listen. There was no way she was going back to that island unless it was by boat.

She glared at him as he assisted her from the chopper. But because her top priority was to leave those lethal wing blades far behind her, she decided to wait before letting him have it. She wanted no chance that he might force her back into that mean machine if she made him so angry, he decided to call the whole day off.

"If you ever, *ever*, *ever* even attempt to put me back in that thing, I will lose all vestiges of civilization and subject you to a quick but agonizing death," she told him, wishing her voice had more thunder and less quiver.

When Crew stopped and looked at her, really looked, she watched his face fall, and all her outrage melted away. Dang the man for actually caring.

"I'm so sorry, Haley. I thought you just had a normal fear of flying, like most people. We'll return by ferry." His sincere apology soothed her, and what was better, she wouldn't have to go back up into the sky!

Haley tried telling herself that her fears were irrational, but she just couldn't let go. Even knowing that the chance of her plummeting to her death in a spiraling, smoking helicopter was almost nonexistent, it would still be her luck to be that one-in-a-whatever number.

"OK. Where are we?" She finally realized that they must have returned to the mainland, but she had no idea what city they were in.

"We're in Long Beach. There are some great boutiques on the island, but I want to take you to some better stores to find a few knockout outfits, and most especially a killer dress," he said.

Haley was worried. She'd been acting like a brat when she told him he'd have to pay, but she knew the prices in some of the stores in this area, and she didn't want to end up blowing ten grand on some glad rags. She'd feel much better just heading to a mall and finding a Macy's. They had great clothes and wouldn't cost her a fortune.

No matter what she'd said on the island, she wasn't making him pay for her clothing.

As he took her hand, leading her to another car, a nice Mercedes GL with a driver holding the back door open, she felt a knot in her stomach. She wouldn't fight with him again unless there was a reason to.

An hour later there was definitely a reason!

*****

"Are you kidding me?! There is no way we are shopping on Rodeo Drive. I may not be the most worldly of people, but I've watched enough movies to know that I can't afford to look at even the *panties* in any of these shops!" Haley thundered.

Crew figured he might want to let the panty comment go. Haley was fit to be tied. Anyway, he found the fire flashing from her eyes rather amusing. He also wanted to get her the perfect dress, and there was no better place than the beautiful and celebrated Rodeo Drive.

"You're not paying, remember? That was the deal," he reminded her.

"I wasn't serious, Crew. I demand that you call the driver back right this minute. I don't think people like me are even allowed to walk in *front* of these stores," she hissed while tapping her foot. "Even though I'm not a hooker with a heart of gold."

Damn, the woman was hot when she was fired up. He could press her against one of the pristine storefront windows right now and take her — well, he could if he were an exhibitionist. And wanted to have his mug shot plastered all over the Smoking Gun website.

The day was warm and her cheeks were flushed, and with her hair slightly mussed, she looked as if she'd just crawled from one hell of a lucky man's bed.

Ignoring her *Pretty Woman* comment, he tried to reason with her. "Look, Haley, I'm on a mission. You can come easy or hard, but this is going to happen. I don't change my mind once it's made up, so what will it be?"

He waited while she seethed. She had no real choice — he'd kidnapped her for the afternoon. He'd just see whether she got over it or threw a tantrum. It was as much a test of her temperament as a mission for the perfect dress, and some indecent lingerie if he could sneak it in.

Finally, she blew out her breath, sent him one final glare, and then uncrossed her arms. It looked as if the battle was over.

"Fine. I'll go, but I insist on paying."

"No."

"Then I'm not doing it." He looked into her eyes to try and intimidate her into backing down, but it wasn't happening. He liked her spunk. However, if she insisted on buying her clothes, he couldn't take her where he'd originally wanted to. He wasn't about to let her stubborn pride break her bank account.

Yes, she'd offered him money to be her teacher, but he'd done a thorough background check on her. She wasn't poor, but she was living off an inheritance from her grandparents and what little money she made at her part-time job while attending school. Since she'd chosen to come on this trip she'd won, she most likely didn't even have the part-time employment any longer. And when this ended, she'd need to make her inheritance last until she was finished with her schooling and could get a decent job.

"Fine." Crew gripped her hand and began strolling down the street with her. Then inspiration hit. His sister's best friend worked in one of the better dress shops. He'd pull her aside and make sure that she gave Haley a believable amount to pay while charging the rest to him. It was win-win for both of them.

Haley didn't look convinced, but she went ahead and allowed him to lead her down the street. With both of them dressed casually, a few people turned up

111

their noses, but he noticed Haley relax when she saw others strolling the beautiful street in similar apparel.

"Not everyone with money is a snob, Haley. That is something you must learn," he said as they approached the store. He needed to discover why she had such a problem with affluent people, why she had such money issues. From the information he'd been able to gleam from her, he knew she'd grown up in a fairly wealthy home. She wasn't poor, by any means. Then again, if she wasn't smart, she could be within a couple years.

As they walked inside, he felt Haley's muscles tense. Then, when Celia popped out and noticed him, her face lit up and she rushed over.

"Crew Storm! What are you doing here?" she squealed as she threw her arms around his neck and gave him a smacking kiss on the lips.

"Careful, Celia. You'll ruin your reputation," he said fondly as he returned her hug.

"I know. I know," she said with a roll of her eyes, before her attention turned toward Haley.

"This is my friend, Haley. We're looking for a few outfits and the perfect evening dress. Not something too over-the-top, but a dress that will make her feel like a million bucks," he said.

Celia's eyes gleamed. "I'd be glad to help you lighten that wallet a bit, Crew."

"I'll be paying," Haley spoke sternly, then realized how rude she was being. "I'm sorry. I'm just a bit nervous. It's nice to meet you."

"Any friend of Crew's is a friend of mine. I've known him since I was five years old. His sister,

Brielle, and I are best friends. I only moved out to California four years ago. Same old sad story of wanting to make it big in Hollywood. Of course, it's never happened." She sighed dramatically, reminding Crew of what an excellent actress she was. "Instead, I'm stuck working in retail, but things could be worse. At least there's a large collection of half-naked men I get to ogle on a daily basis."

At those words, he felt Haley relax. He knew being around Celia would do the trick. She was a sweet girl, always had been. She needed to focus more, that was all. At one point, he'd been sure she and Tanner would end up together, but it had just never happened.

The next hour was a blur as Celia grabbed a variety of outfits, making Haley try each one on, then shaking her head every time. He had to agree. Sure, she looked nice in all of them, but none of them called to him yet. He wanted something that would pop. Though he didn't know exactly what he was looking for, once it was found, he'd just know.

He was looking down, reading the New York Times, when Celia cleared her throat. Haley stood before him with three-inch heels and a shimmering teal gown. The top hugged her tight, with thin straps holding it in place, and accented her scrumptious breasts. The dress molded to her body until just below her hips, where it flared slightly, then stopped four inches above her knees.

"Perfect," he said out loud, his tongue nearly hanging from his mouth.

At his words, Haley grinned while doing a full spin and he got his first mouthwatering glance at her bare and exquisitely toned back. No fabric blocked his view, and as his eyes dipped lower, he itched to run his fingers over the top of the material, which rested just above the curve of her perfectly rounded backside.

"We'll take it!" There was no question. This was the dress.

"That's what I thought as soon as I saw her in it," Celia sighed dreamily. "The shoes are perfect, too."

"I couldn't agree more. Now, where do we go for lingerie, Celia?" Crew asked.

Haley flushed as she turned to him in surprise. His own question was taking him by surprise, too. The thought of her in a garter belt and stockings with nothing else on but those heels had him shifting in his seat. Oh yes, they were lingerie shopping. He would certainly work in a lesson that involved her modeling the sheer lace and garters for him. Before too much longer, he would be taking this game to a whole new level.

"You must go to Agent Provocateur. No woman can wear any of their pieces without feeling like an absolute sex goddess," Celia insisted as she led Haley to the back.

When it came time to pay, he slipped Celia his credit card, feeling a tad guilty about the deception, but if Haley had known the true cost of the dress, she'd have had a minor stroke. Never had he thought about money before the day his father had told him that his inheritance and trust fund were being taken away. He'd always just had plenty of it. Life as a billionaire's kid…

That first year of being on his own, however, had taught him a lot. He no longer took wealth for granted, and he now knew how important it could be for someone who didn't have much. But there were some items that were worth splurging on. The perfect dress was one of them.

Surprisingly, Haley didn't fight him on the panties. She was entranced from the moment they entered Agent Provocateur. The only problem he had was her refusal to allow him to give her his opinion.

In this store, he wasn't able to slip in his credit card. Haley wouldn't even let him know the amount. He knew it wouldn't be cheap, but he'd figure out a way to make it right with her, soften the financial blow.

They passed the next couple of hours purchasing a few more outfits, now at less expensive boutiques, and enjoying the beautiful California sunshine. When dusk arrived, Crew led Haley back to Long Beach, where this time they boarded a private boat for the twenty-two-mile ride to the island.

"You are both in luck tonight. The dolphins have been entertaining the guests."

"Ooh, I love dolphins. I have been meaning to take one of the tours offered on the island, but haven't had a chance yet. I must do it before I have to leave. I can't believe I have only a little over a week left," Haley said with a frown.

Crew's gut clenched at her words. He'd known her for less than a week and already he was growing attached in a strange way. She was just so full of life, so full of happiness. Her enthusiasm for everything around her was contagious.

Halfway to the island, they saw the dolphins dancing on the water next to the boat, showing off for Crew and Haley as the captain slowed so they could enjoy the show a little longer.

The sun was just starting to set and Crew couldn't fight the urge to slip his arm around Haley's shoulders and pull her tightly against his side. And when she looked up, he couldn't resist bending down and capturing her lips for just the briefest of moments.

As she sighed into his mouth, he felt his wavering control snap. They would make fireworks ignite when they finally came together — it couldn't be soon enough.

Chapter Thirteen

As she walked from the elevator, Haley felt a twinge of her old insecurities. Here she was in a stunning gown with her hair piled atop her head and with her newly acquired makeup lightly applied. She'd even spritzed herself with the subtly scented bottle of perfume she'd found in the bathroom with a ribbon tied on top. This was what she wanted. She wanted to turn heads. She wanted to feel gorgeous.

So why was everything inside of her telling her to turn around and run back to her room? She wanted to hide away and slip back into a baggy T-shirt and frayed shorts.

But refusing to let her fears dictate her actions, Haley moved purposefully through the lobby toward the softly lit bar where Marlin was working. Crew had only instructed her to meet him at ten at the bar; all she knew was that he was taking her to a nice dinner. If only she could feel a little less afraid, a little more excited.

"Wowee! You look hot!" Haley looked up to find Marlin giving her an exaggerated wink. "Beautiful ladies get the first-class bar stool," he finished as he came around the bar and pulled out the seat for her.

"Why, thank you, kind sir," she replied demurely. She sat as gracefully as she could, but getting comfortable took her a few moments, what with adjusting her dress and positioning her heels just right on the rungs of the stool.

"Would you like a surprise or would a woman of your high class like a glass of champagne?"

"You may surprise me. And you can quit that flattery any time, Marlin. You're making me blush," she whispered as she looked over her shoulder. The bar was crowded, but luckily the crowd was near the new piano player and the large gas fireplace on the other side of the room, and no one was paying the two of them the least bit of attention.

"Hey, a dress that hot, covering a body that's even hotter, deserves some of my special attention."

"I'm going to tell your wife," she said. "In fact, she's right over there."

Marlin looked around in terror, causing Haley's nerves to fade away into laughter. She was glad Crew wasn't there yet — it gave her a few necessary moments to relax.

"I was just having some fun. That was downright cruel," he pouted as he began mixing her a drink.

"Don't mess with a woman in heels, Marlin. You'll lose every time," she said, still laughing.

"Don't I know it," he sighed as he placed a martini in front of her. She raised her eyebrows at the choice, but picked up the amusingly retro silver-plated cocktail stick and started moving it and its olives around in the glass. "I figure you're dressed classy, so you need a classy drink," he offered.

"I see. So when I'm in my cutoffs, I get the Bottom-Feeder Special?"

"I'd never think of doing that to you, missy. Do you want me to slip you some brazini with fennel puree? It's delicious."

"I would love some, but I'm meeting Crew here and he's taking me out to dinner." She was thinking the brazini sounded much better, though.

"That explains the new dress. I knew the boss man would get his claws into you. He has an eye for the pretty ladies."

"It's not like that. He's helping me out — and though he's a pain in the butt, I have to admit that he's doing a pretty good job so far," she admitted.

"Mmm, that's what I like to hear. You smell divine." Haley tensed all over again as Crew's mouth descended on her neck and he took a gentle bite from her skin. She instantly felt goose bumps and found herself fighting the urge to lean into the firmness of his chest when he pressed his body against her back.

"You're not supposed to eavesdrop," she said when she found her voice again.

"Haven't you heard that it's not nice to talk about people behind their backs?" he countered.

"We were just discussing my upcoming mystery date," she defended.

119

"Speaking of which, everything is ready. I'm sorry to keep you waiting. My sister was on the phone and no matter how many times I tried, I couldn't get her off the line. *Melodrama* is Brielle's middle name."

"Is she OK?"

"Yes, she's fine. It's just family theater, and Brielle has bitten off a bit more than she can chew. It's actually kind of enjoyable. She's always been the baby and quite spoiled. I am going to have to visit her soon, just to see how her ranch is working out."

"Did you say *ranch*?" Haley asked.

"I did indeed."

"OK. You are *definitely* going to have to give me more details. I want to know how a wealthy member of the Storm family ends up working right in the dirt."

"How do you know I'm wealthy?" he asked with a smirk. Haley rolled her eyes.

"Well, let's see, maybe it's all the magazine articles, *or* the charities your family donates to. It might *possibly* be the over-the-top resort that you run. *Nah*, it's the Rolex." She laughed as she placed her arm through his so he could lead her away. "Night, Marlin," she called back before they made their exit.

To Haley's surprise, Crew started leading her not out the resort's front doors but toward the back. Yet she made no comment as the two of them walked side by side toward the ornate patio doors behind an elegant sitting area. A violinist was playing for a small crowd of people sipping wine and eating a variety of cheeses and fruits. This place was amazing.

They stepped through the doors onto the candlelit patio, an area she hadn't seen before. Large fire pits were strategically placed with lounge chairs surrounding them, and plants and trees were positioned to offer privacy for each grouping. Hearing light laughter and happy voices in the different nooks, Haley started imagining passionate embraces, drugging kisses, and racing hearts.

"I'm so happy to be dining here, Crew," she said quietly. "You've done well."

"I'm glad you think so." His eyes captured hers in an intense gaze, and her heart nearly stalled as she continued walking beside him. Being fully aware that she was getting too caught up in the moment didn't help her heart flutter any less. This wasn't going according to plan, but she was having a hard time caring.

When the path ended, she gasped at the sight of a rich red carpet laid out upon the sand. As she looked up at him, her vision seemed to fog momentarily. What lesson could he be trying to teach her now?

Without giving her a moment to breathe, he led her down the carpet to a golden cabana only about ten yards from the gently lapping water of the warm Pacific Ocean. Beneath the structure was a table for two. The only illumination inside was a string of twinkling lights overhead, casting a soft, intimate glow.

She sighed as he showed her to one of the chairs, which easily slid out from the table on the hard, clear floor of the cabana. The glass was almost like a window on the beach floor, giving the feeling of sitting directly on the sand without sinking into it.

After pushing her chair in and dropping a light kiss on the back of her neck, he sat across from her, and within seconds a waiter appeared and opened a bottle of wine, presenting it to Crew for his approval.

"I hope you don't mind, Haley, but I've ordered our dinner. Would you care for a glass of Pouilly-Fuissé? It will taste like nothing you've tried before."

Haley nodded with wide, curious eyes, taking the long-stemmed glass and sampling the crisp white liquid, smelling tantalizingly of fruit and oak. The explosion of flavors in her mouth was divine. The only wine she'd drunk before came out of a cheap supercenter store bottle. She couldn't drink that stuff again — not after this.

The waiter set down a dish, and left them. Crew dipped a silver spoon in the small bowl, and slipped something onto a buttered toast point, then lifted it to her lips. Without even thinking of saying no, she took a bite, then wrinkled her nose at the salty flavor.

"I don't like that," she said, quickly swallowing it down, and then taking a large gulp of her wine. Crew laughed as he took a big bite of his own portion and hummed in pleasure.

"Not everyone cares for caviar, even Golden Osetra," he said with a smile. "People always say that it's an acquired taste."

Not one I'd like to acquire, Haley muttered to herself and hoped the meal improved from this point on. Things did look up when the waiter set down their next course, asparagus salad with brilliant roasted red peppers.

"What is the lesson in all of this, Crew? I don't want to sound ungrateful, because this is by far the most romantic evening I've ever had in my life, but I am curious why you're doing all of this," she finally asked.

"This is how a woman should be treated, Haley. She should be worshipped, wined and dined. When a beautiful lady takes the time to put on a stunning gown, she needs to be given the royal treatment. Men will fall all over themselves just for a chance to be in their woman's presence. The lesson in this is to teach you what your expectation should be in how a man treats you. If you want to attract your man, you first need to feel that you're worthy of attracting him. A night of romance should be deserved. When a man truly wants you, there is no limit to what he will do for nothing more than an evening in your presence."

The deep baritone of his voice, and the words he uttered, held Haley spellbound. Was she beautiful? As she'd looked in the mirror at the glimmering teal gown, she'd felt...different, more attractive. But would she go so far as to say she was beautiful? No one had ever told her she was — certainly not her grandparents — so how could she think that of herself?

She wanted to believe the light in his eyes was real, but could it all be just an act? He'd refused to take payment from her for being her teacher, but was this all a game to him? She couldn't fault him for that, but what if he were setting her up, planning to rip her apart? She might never heal, might never have the confidence in herself that she so desperately sought.

"I can see the doubt in your eyes; it's your biggest weakness. You have to have faith in yourself. You asked me to teach you how to seduce a man, but it's not an answer I can give you. The way you seduce a man is by having confidence in yourself. Remember what I told you? It doesn't matter if you are slim, athletic or curvy. It doesn't matter the color of your hair or eyes. Nothing matters except for you knowing that you are sexy. If you look into a man's eyes and let him know you are too good for him, then you own him. The most important rule is that you are what you believe you are, so be careful how you feel about yourself."

The truth was shining in his eyes as he spoke. Haley could see he wasn't playing a game with her, he wasn't lying just to make her his slave. Was it really that simple? Could she just believe she was a prize to be won, and suddenly have any man she wanted — at least if she really wanted him enough?

The waiter slipped in and took away her barely touched salad as he set down their next course, seared sea scallops with spring onion soubise. Though the smell was heavenly, she was too lost in Crew's eyes to pay attention to the food.

"We'll have more on this lesson after our meal, while we're sitting by the fire. I've had my chef prepare this especially for you, and I want you to enjoy the entire experience," Crew said and took a bite.

Finally freed from his gaze, Haley speared a scallop and slipped it inside her mouth, then purred in pleasure. It practically melted on her tongue. Crew kept the conversation more light as they finished their main course.

The last drop was drank from the exquisite bottle, the wine having helped Haley's confidence to grow, and the waiter laid out their dessert and set a new bottle down at their table. Her first bite of beignets with coffee pots de crème was almost an out-of-body experience. But, still, it was hard to enjoy the meal, no matter how good, when she was in a constant state of arousal — something very new for her inexperienced body.

"So, tell me how your sister managed to end up on a ranch," she asked between small bites. She wanted to prolong the bliss.

"I don't want to bore you during our date," he hedged.

"I promise that you won't."

"Well, don't say that I didn't warn you," he said with a chuckle. "A couple of years ago, my siblings and I were…I guess the word would be *spoiled*."

"You? Spoiled?" she gasped dramatically, then smiled. "I simply can't imagine."

"OK, yes, I was spoiled. This is about Brielle, not me, though," he said with his twinkling eyes crinkling at the corners.

"Sorry. I will behave," she said.

"Anyway, my father decided to teach us a lesson. We would lose our inheritance and trust funds if we didn't play by his rules. That, of course, left us little

125

choice but to do what he asked of us, but we were all resentful, thinking there was nothing that needed changing in our lives."

"Do you still feel bitter toward your father?"

"No. About six months into this project my resentment faded, and I realized he was right. We *had* become spoiled brats — of no use to society at all. I will deny that if you repeat it, though," he said.

"My lips are sealed."

"Well, the task was to take a failing business and make it a success." She waited for him to go on, but he picked up his glass and took a sip of wine.

"How did you end up with the resort and your sister get landed with a ranch?"

"My father set down five folders and told us to fight among ourselves over which failing business we would take. My sister was horrified, and she refused to even look at the various operations. By the time she came around and decided a life of poverty wasn't for her, the ranch was all that was left. Let's just say that she threw a fit, and tried to bribe, cajole, and blackmail each of us to trade. No one would. So, long story short, she was stuck with the ranch."

"And how does she feel now?" Haley thought she'd get along really well with Crew's father. He sounded like a good man.

"She won't admit it to our father, but she loves it. Her first week there, she called me ten times a day in tears, telling me nothing was worth what she was going through, but after a few months, the calls started coming in less often. I had my doubts that she would see it through, but I am very proud of her now. She's grown more than the rest of us, I believe."

"She sounds like a good woman."

"She is now. Without a doubt, she was once a self-centered little witch, but this lesson has changed all of us for the better, and probably Brielle the most. My siblings and I are closer than we have been since we were small kids, and this last Christmas was the first time we all got together because we wanted to, and not because we were obligated to. It has changed us, and I am grateful to my father for giving us a swift kick in the derrière," Crew said with a small smile.

This man before her was strong as solid steel, both with his love of his family and his complete focus on helping a stranger. He was also kind and gentle when he needed to be, loyal and compassionate. How could Haley help but fall for him? She knew it was a deadly error. But she didn't know how to pull back, how to lock down emotions that she'd never felt before. Somehow, she must try. Could she just focus on Walker?...Who? She couldn't even seem to picture the face of the man who was the reason she'd begun this entire process.

A peaceful silence surrounded them as they continued eating, both of them lost in their own thoughts. She just hoped Crew never became a mind reader, because she didn't want to reveal so much about herself.

When they'd taken their last bite, Crew led her to a couple of lounge chairs placed side by side, with a fire burning in a pit off to the side, keeping a dim glow of light around them. Haley slipped off her shoes, and the sand felt soft and cool as it slid between her toes. As she looked around, she realized they were completely alone. This must be his own personal area.

Haley lay back on one of the chairs, enjoying the soft breeze blowing over her, and she felt Crew's hand move gently across her stomach, sending butterflies fluttering from the pit of her stomach to her toes and back.

"Seduce me, Haley," he whispered.

She turned her head, her eyes suddenly heavy as she looked at him.

"I don't know how. You're supposed to teach me," she murmured.

"Seduce me," he repeated, heat flaring between them.

"I can't…" she trailed off.

"Seduce me."

Something inside her came alive and her body moved. She didn't know what she was doing, but somehow nature took over and it became all about quenching the fire within her.

Chapter Fourteen

Crew watched the flare in her eyes as she made her decision. There was passion in those green depths, but there was also grit and determination. She was done being a wallflower and was ready to explore what was locked within the deepest realms of her being.

As difficult as it was for him to keep his hands to himself, he lay back and waited. She needed to break free, and for her to do that, she had to escape from her shell. He wouldn't let it go too far, not far enough that she'd have regrets. He would just let her see what effect she had on him.

After their last course, he'd dismissed his waitstaff, to eliminate the chance of interruption. He could now give her a hands-on lesson of what a woman could do to a man. Damn but he was attracted to her, and that was a problem for his noble plan. He never would have believed that this was the same woman who'd stepped into his life on a sidewalk and offered him money.

She'd already grown, and now it was time for him to show her exactly how much.

Lifting the fabric of her skirt above her knees, Haley moved over, straddling his lap and positioning her luscious round behind right against his rapidly growing erection. A groan escaped from his throat, and she smiled in victory.

Watching her expressions as she tentatively moved her hips in a slow circle was about the sexiest damned thing he'd ever witnessed in his life. He was certain he wouldn't survive her exploration.

"What do I do?" she asked as her hands rested on his chest. He wouldn't tell her. She had to listen to what her body was demanding of her. She needed to let go of her inhibitions and dance to the beat of her heart.

"You need to seduce me. Make me think of no woman other than you," he whispered.

She tensed as if unsure of the next step, then slowly bent forward. He almost breathed out in relief as her lips neared his. He wanted to taste her flavor, devour her mouth. But she kissed only the corner of his lips before moving on to his chin.

When her mouth trailed delicate kisses along his jaw, and then her tongue smoothed its way along his neck, his erection jumped painfully as it tried to escape the confines of his slacks. She could obviously feel his excitement, because she pushed her hips harder against him as the two of them played a very dangerous game.

No longer able to refrain from touching her, Crew lifted his hands and ran them through the strands of her soft blond hair. Pulling out the clips and band holding it captive, he sighed as her hair cascaded down, creating a glowing curtain between her face and his body.

Haley leaned up, and he wanted to protest as her mouth left his skin, but then her shaking fingers moved to the top button of his shirt, and his heart stopped for a moment before it resumed with a pounding intensity.

One by one, she undid his buttons until the material fell to his sides. Then her fingernails scraped along the light brushing of hair on his chest and she drew patterns on his skin, then circled his hard nipples.

When she bent down and ran her tongue over the tanned skin of his chest, his back arched off the lounge chair.

She was learning quickly. He was going to have to end this soon — before he couldn't.

Just as he was getting ready to tell her, *Good job, you've succeeded in seducing me*, her lips traveled lower and the hot breath from her mouth was now on his stomach. No words could possibly escape his tight throat.

When he thought she'd stop, her hand drifted lower, running across the hardness begging to be set free. She glided her skillful fingers across the head of his clothes-covered arousal and he could feel himself losing control. When she took care of his button and zipper, his sanity flew out the window.

He knew he should stop this — knew this wasn't part of the deal — but he was human, after all. Thank heavens, he always had protection on him, whether he planned on sex or not. It was just something instilled in him — the old Boy Scout motto. Before he lost his mind altogether — along with his pants — he grabbed the foil packet from his pocket and clutched it tightly within his palm.

The first tentative swipe of her tongue along the tip of his arousal was the last of his undoing. His mind went blank as she worked her innocent magic. When she sucked him into the warm recesses of her mouth, he saw stars.

Mission accomplished.

He enjoyed the unbelievable pleasure of her mouth fully around his head for a few more moments before he couldn't take any more without embarrassing himself.

"My turn," he gasped, then sat up and grabbed her by the hips, quickly pulling her up his body so she was sitting on his lap.

"You taste salty and sweet, silky…yet so hard. I want to do that some more."

Her enthusiasm had him throbbing to the point of madness.

"Baby, you can do it plenty more later, but right now, *I* need to taste *you*," he said before pulling her to him and finally closing his mouth over hers. As his tongue slipped inside her warm mouth, he knew he just couldn't get enough. Nothing was enough.

Not deep enough.

Not long enough.

Not fast enough.

Not slow enough.

Not enough of her open to his touch.

His hands found the clasp behind her neck and he quickly undid it before sliding her straps down her naked back and finding the zipper to undo the skirt of her dress. Within seconds, her bare breasts pressed against his naked chest.

As her hard nipples rubbed against his skin, she groaned into his mouth, and rubbed her hips against him. Lifting her dress, he quickly pulled it up over her head and tossed it aside, then raised his hips and thrust down his pants. The only thing keeping him from entering her was an incredibly small piece of black lace.

As his erection throbbed against her — *so hot!* — he decided he'd better change positions fast before he plunged in and satisfied only himself. She'd done her job of seducing him; now it was his turn to seduce her.

Haley gasped to find herself on her back, looking up at Crew whose frame was enveloped in the black night sky with speckled brilliant stars surrounding him like an aura. Crew smiled down at her, excitement shuddering through him. Kissing her again, he lay on top of her, enjoying the way her soft curves held him just right.

As she pushed her hips up toward him, her body telling him exactly what she desired, he moved his mouth down her throat, taking a moment to feel her excited pulse against his tongue as her blood raced.

His first taste of her dusky nipples was magical, and he sucked her deep within his mouth as she groaned her approval. Lavishing her breasts with nips, kisses, flicks of his tongue and the stroke of his fingers while her hands fisted in his hair, Crew felt on the verge of breaking.

But only when he had made her come would he take his own pleasure. As he continued fondling her generous breasts with one hand, he moved the other one downward, easily ripping away her panties, then slipping a finger inside her wet heat.

When his thumb began stroking her swollen womanhood, she bucked against his hand, her breathing shallow, panting. He bit down gently on her nipple as he flicked his thumb across her tender flesh below, and then moved up just in time to capture her scream with his lips as her body released, his fingers saturated with her orgasm.

Before she was finished, Crew barely managed to sheath himself before he opened her legs wide and positioned himself.

"Open your eyes," he demanded, barely recognizing his own strained voice.

When Haley could open them just enough for him to see how she was feeling, he plunged fully inside her, nearly exploding as her tight skin closed around him.

Before he pulled back to plunge in again, the pain on her face registered somewhere in his mind. Her mouth gaped open as her nails dug into the skin of his arms.

Crew was so shocked, he couldn't seem to move. *She was a virgin*. It was evident by the tightness, the pain crossing her features, the shocked look on her face.

"Why? How?" He whispered as he stilled, staying connected inside her.

"Ouch," was her reply.

Noble? Ha. He felt decidedly unheroic.

Finally regaining a semblance of control, Crew tenderly pulled out of her, then reached below the lounge chair and grabbed a blanket he'd placed there earlier.

He turned on his back and pulled her tightly against him, then covered them both. His body was still throbbing dangerously — could he be risking permanent damage? — but he wouldn't go on until she talked to him, explained.

She'd just given him something so special, a gift indescribably sacred. The least he could give her in return was a chance to adjust. The one thing he wouldn't give her was freedom.

In a blink of an eye, she'd just become his, and there was no way he was teaching her how to seduce another man. She was his now, only his.

Chapter Fifteen

As Haley lay in Crew's arms, his hand rubbed soothingly up and down her back. He said nothing while she sorted through the varying emotions filling her heart and whirling in her mind. She was in a bit of shock, a little pain, and a lot of pleasure.

Her body was aching, but the burning had already gone away, and now she was more filled with confusion than anything else. She'd never before been with a man, and yet his soft whisperings of *seduce me* had made her turn into a wanton.

Hadn't her grandmother once told her that all women were whores? She'd said that Haley's mother had been a whore and that's why she'd gotten pregnant. She'd blamed Haley's mother for being a whore, and blamed Haley for being alive. Haley was an abomination that never should have been born, and it was all because of sex. *Lord, just remembering those bitter tirades the few times her grandmother even deigned to speak to her sent her thoughts tumbling over each other wildly.*

Even knowing all of this, Haley had still lain with a man, was still lying across his chest. She might not be fifteen, as her mother had been, but she hadn't once thought about protection. His words *seduce me* had melted her from the inside out, and instinct had drowned out all rational thought. Her body had reached blindly for relief. And she'd felt relief in spades, though Crew hadn't.

How could something that felt so wonderful be wrong? What if her grandmother was wrong? The world would end if people didn't make new children, wouldn't it? So sex couldn't be the evil thing her grandmother had taught her it was. The old woman had obviously had sex herself. Haley had never thought to question whether her grandmother thought of herself as a whore too. Maybe the old hypocrite had only done it that one time out of duty. It wouldn't surprise Haley a bit.

As Haley lay in Crew's arms, she didn't feel shame, she felt…something indescribable. She felt safe and comforted. She felt as if what she was doing was right.

"Talk to me, Haley. Why wouldn't you tell me you are a virgin?" When she was silent, he continued. "I didn't mean for this to go so far…at least not tonight. I just wanted you to see how desirable you are." He stopped as a deep sigh emerged from within his chest and vibrated through her body. "There's

137

obviously no problem there, because you made me lose my mind. I'm still burning for you, though I know I shouldn't be. Yes, you are an amazing seductress."

Curiosity to see whether he was telling the truth made Haley move. Her hand slid down his chest, past his stomach, which quivered at her touch, and then over his still-sheathed manhood, which, true to his word, was hard as stone.

Fearlessly, she cupped her hand around his thick shaft and gently squeezed it.

"Haley…" he warned. "I'm trying to get this to go away…" His sentence ended on a moan.

But she didn't want it to go away; she wanted him to experience the same firestorm of feeling that she had.

"I'm sorry I didn't tell you. I wasn't expecting… I mean, I didn't think we'd…" Her words trailed off.

"If you keep stroking me like that, I'm not going to be able to remain a gentleman," he warned.

Instead of backing off, she tightened her fingers around him and moved her hand down, and then up again around the head of his arousal.

"Haley," he groaned as he lifted his head and gently took her lips in his. She didn't hesitate, clasping onto his supple mouth and accepting the caress of his lips, her hands finally moving from his shaft only so she could clasp his head.

He shifted so they were lying side by side beneath the blanket, his hand rising to enclose her breast, stirring the ever burning coals of desire in her stomach. She felt a pulsing throb begin in her core, as if begging to have him within her body again.

Fear of the pain of his entry was fading as one of his hands rubbed her swollen nipples, and the other ran along her back and then down to grip her enticing behind. She wiggled in his grasp, not able to get close enough to him.

More. She needed more.

"We shouldn't do this. I don't want to hurt you," he warned.

"Everybody does this, and the slight pain is so worth the pleasure," she countered.

With a moan, Crew slowly turned her onto her back, leaned over and kissed her until she was breathless, then sucked her bottom lip into his mouth. Her hips lifted, seeking his touch.

His fingers moved down her stomach, and then, using the moistness from her body, he rubbed his fingers over that oh-so-pleasurable-spot, drawing out her lustful cry. Just as she was tightening, getting ready to fall headlong over that wonderful cliff again, he pulled back and her cries now voiced her protest.

A low chuckle at her impatience rumbled through his chest. "Let's go over the edge together," he said as he slid over her, his body once again poised above hers, the head of his impressive arousal resting in the cradle of her thighs.

Yes. That was what she wanted. She wanted to fly with him, to soar away into paradise.

Far more controlled, Crew slid a couple inches inside her heat, her body stretching to accommodate him. She felt just the slightest pinch of discomfort, but he apparently could read her body better than she could, because he was slow and easy as he pushed in inch by beautiful inch.

By the time his hips were flush against hers, all Haley could feel was a pulsing need for him to move, to stoke the flames of burning desire that were radiating through her. He stilled as she wrapped her legs around his back, and tugged on him with her hands.

She might have been inexperienced, but her body was having no trouble telling her what she needed. Her limbs were moving as if they had a brain of their own.

"I'm trying to be careful, Haley," he groaned as she continued tugging on him.

"Take me, Crew. Please, now," she begged. "I need you."

Watching his eyes flash with need, she cried out as he began to move, slowly and steadily, in and out of her heat, causing her body to throb.

Closer.

Higher.

Faster.

She was so close to exploding. She needed more, just a little more. Playing her like a master, he sped up, his body hitting against hers in all the right places.

"Your body is so sexy, Haley. I want to be deep within your folds all day and night. The curve of your hips in my hand, the slickness of your heat encircling me." Crew breathed heavily as he continued to thrust inside her.

Haley couldn't form words, could only groan as he lifted her higher, his words pushing her even closer to the edge of glory.

Her tender breasts ached as they rubbed against his solid chest, her body fully enflamed.

Just as she felt him tense, felt his body stiffen, and his shaft began pulsing against the walls of her core, Haley flew apart, her body gripping him tight as she spiraled down a long tunnel into a dark abyss.

The first explosion had been wondrous and eye-opening; this one beggared speech. Crew stilled above her as the two of them flew down the mountain, their orgasms sapping their last ounce of energy. Haley barely registered the movement as he pulled from her body and shifted their positions so she was once again lying in his arms.

"Thank you for such a gift," he murmured.

She didn't understand what he was talking about, but she was embarrassed at her inexperience and didn't want him to realize how very little she knew of love.

"Why haven't you slept with a man before?" he pressed on.

This she could answer. "I told you when I met you that I wanted to learn to seduce a man. I didn't know how." It was pretty simple.

"Just because you don't know how to seduce a man doesn't mean men aren't chasing after you," he said, the soothing feel of the tips of his fingers continuing to lazily trail up and down her spine, added to her relaxation in his arms.

"I don't want you to know who I really am." The thought terrified her. She was comfortable, sated, happy in this moment. She didn't want it ever to end. Didn't want her past to spoil the mood for either of them.

"Please tell me." He wasn't demanding answers but seemed honestly to want to know.

If he ran screaming, then at least she could say she'd learned a lot about herself. There was a burning need inside her to tell him, to let him inside her childhood heartbreak. She hadn't really had anyone else to talk to before, no one like a friend. Wasn't it supposed to be therapeutic to get things off your chest?

Here goes, she thought, as she started to let the story pour out.

"My mother was only fifteen when she got pregnant with me. She was from a very affluent family and her parents were furious when they found out, but she'd kept it hidden so long that they couldn't force her to get an abortion. Her parents told her she was a sinner and would burn in hell. I was born a month early and there were severe complications and she ended up bleeding to death on the table," she began.

"Oh, Haley, I'm so sorry…" he said, but she held a finger to his mouth. If she was going to get through this, she couldn't have him interrupting, or she'd fall apart.

"Both of my grandparents thought I was an abomination, a sin come to life. They were ashamed of my mother, but some of their so-called friends had

142

found out about me, so they couldn't give me up for adoption or they risked shame upon their family. They were stuck with a baby they didn't want and hated to look at."

"Haley —" he tried again, sighing and tightening his arms around her in comfort.

"They hired a nanny and solidified the truth that they didn't ever really want to know me. The only time I ever even saw them was when they came to tell me how terribly I was doing, or what a disappointment I was. I grew up with the servants, who were kind to me, taking me under their wing and teaching me all I needed to know. My grandparents didn't send me to school until I was old enough for boarding school, and then only did that so I'd be out of their house and they wouldn't have a constant reminder in front of them of the shame their daughter had brought upon them." Haley paused to wait for the lump to go away.

Crew said nothing, just gently stroked her back and waited for her to continue.

"I was so ashamed of who I was, even though the servants tried for years to tell me that my grandparents were wrong. Many of them stayed on only so they could look out for me when I was home during school holidays, and I'm grateful they did. It's why it's so much easier for me to speak with people in the service industry. I was never to show my face when my grandparents were entertaining guests. They didn't want to remind the community that I was around. They'd done their duty by providing a roof

143

over my head and food, but that was as far as they were willing to go.

"How was school? Did it give you freedom?"

"No. School was worse than home. My grandparents paid my tuition and gave me the bare minimum of supplies and clothing, but I was going to a wealthy school where all of the other kids had plenty of money to spend on activities and socializing. I had nothing and was left behind. They all looked at me like a charity case, and I made zero friends while there. It was lonely, of course. I always was. I became interested in boys even though I had my grandmother's voice in my head calling me a slut for even thinking about wanting to kiss one of them."

"She was wrong!"

"I know that now. I honestly do, but it took me years. My grandparents died when I was eighteen. There was a gas leak in the house and they passed in their sleep. Even though they were horrible to me, I still felt sadness. None of the servants died —they slept in separate quarters behind the house. They've moved on, and we've now lost touch. A couple checked on me for a couple of years after the death of my grandparents, but then they had to worry about their own lives. The house sits empty, only a gardener left to make sure the grass doesn't overtake it."

"So, you've held on to it for six years?"

"I haven't sold it yet. I honestly don't know why. It took over a year for all the estate to finalize and for me to get my inheritance since there wasn't a will. I have always planned on getting rid of it. There are no happy memories there for me now, I just haven't done it yet. I will..."

"I don't know how I can make any of this better for you, Haley. I can't even say that I understand, because I don't. It's inconceivable for me to think of people treating one of their own kin, someone they are supposed to love, in that heartless, inhuman way."

Silence stretched out between them as she tried to push her raw emotions down. She'd shared her tale with only one other person, her counselor at college, and it had helped her to see she wasn't a child of Satan who didn't deserve to live. Still, it wasn't easy to get beyond the horrors of her early life.

She hated admitting all of this to Crew, since she wanted him to view her as something more than a child in the shadows, but it also felt good to get it off her chest, to share this burden with another human being, one who wasn't being paid to listen. As much as speaking with her counselor had helped, the woman had just sat behind her desk taking notes, hadn't rubbed Haley's back and let her know it would all be OK. Still, without her, Haley would never have had the confidence to get a job or take this vacation she'd won, or ever been able to approach Crew to ask for his help.

It had taken her years to gain the courage to try to change who she was. She wanted to find a man who would look at her, desire her, maybe even love her. Every romantic movie she'd watched had a hero racing in to save the day, and she'd ached for that, whether it was politically correct or not. She wanted her prince charming to save her.

"So, you decided to change your life, and then you found me."

"No. Not quite that quickly. It took me years to work up the courage to actually find a man to teach me," she admitted. "I came here because I won the trip, and I figured this was a good place to find a teacher because it's an island — much harder for a man to escape," she finished with a laugh.

"I don't want to escape you." The words sounded wonderful, but she wasn't stupid. They were both caught up in this magical night — in this surreal moment. They would probably both see things in another light once dawn approached.

"You are teaching me to feel different about myself, Crew. I've felt things in the last week that I never imagined I would, but this is all just a fantasy, a game I came up with to change who I am. It may work, and it may not, but I don't want to think past right now. I *need* to remain in reality." She pleaded with him to understand. "Let's not pretend this is something it isn't."

After a short pause, he responded. "I will agree to live in the moment if you agree to quit the game and give me a chance. I'm not a bad guy, and though it surprises me to say this, I like you, Haley…a lot. Let's forget about this other man you wanted to seduce, and focus on having you seduce only me from now on. You're pretty damned great at it!"

Haley knew there was a reason she should protest — knew she'd figure out what that reason was if she thought about it long enough, but while his hands caressed her, while his warmth kept her sated and

146

secure, she couldn't find fault with what he was asking of her. After a brief pause, she nodded her head.

"Say it, Haley." The nod wasn't good enough.

"I will forget the other guy…for now." She knew her answer wasn't good enough for Crew, but at least he wasn't pushing her.

The two of them lay in each other's arms for the next hour, or two — they didn't know — listening to the soothing sound of the ocean waves until the cool evening air had them admitting it was time to go in. When Crew led her to his room that night, she didn't fight him. She wasn't ready to let go just yet.

Pulling her into his arms to hold her and nothing more, she felt the first warm stirrings in her untutored heart. But she couldn't be falling in love with him. She didn't know what love was, had no examples of it in her life. Her emotions were clearly just in overdrive from everything that had occurred during the day, and night.

Falling asleep with a smile on her face and Crew's arms wrapped around her, she slept better than she ever had before.

Chapter Sixteen

"Wake up. We're going to one of my favorite places for lunch."

Haley felt as if one-ton weights were pressed against her eyelids. Wake up? No way. She was warm, sated, very sore, and unwilling ever to climb from bed again. Maybe if she ignored him, he'd eventually go away. It was worth a shot.

"Pretending to be asleep won't do you any good. It's already noon. I've gotten in four hours of work and a ten-mile jog on the beach, plus I calmed down my sister on a half-hour-long phone call."

Crew was sounding way too cheery. "Show-off," she muttered under her breath. She wanted to throw one pillow at his face, and bury her head underneath another one. She wasn't budging.

"Haley, I can see your muscles tensing. I know you're awake."

"I wouldn't be if you'd kindly shut up," she grumbled, savagely twisting her body away from the sound of his voice and snuggling down deeper into the softness of his mattress.

Normally, Haley was a very happy person in the mornings, but she'd stayed up long into the night. And anyway, accomplished seductresses needed their beauty rest.

"I'm taking you to my favorite place on the island to eat. Now get up," he said before playfully swatting her on her bare behind. She was so shocked, she sat up in bed, clutching the sheet to her chest, her eyes wide as she looked into his smiling face.

This wasn't the same man she'd met a week before.

"I saw and tasted your luscious curves last night...twice. Why hide them now?" he asked as he sat on the bed and ran his finger along the top of the sheet in an attempt to free it from her grip.

"That was...well, that was..." She didn't know what she wanted to say.

"Something we will do again and again," he finished for her.

Haley was in shock. She hadn't known what to expect this morning, but certainly not this playful, lighthearted Crew. She had expected him to look at her with pity, or not look at her at all, having made his conquest.

"That wasn't our deal," she finally said as her fingers clung to the silken sheet — her only protection at the moment. She had a sudden desire to

149

slip into one of her baggy tops and hide away for the next week.

"The deal has changed," he answered her simply. "If you keep gazing at me with those wide, innocent eyes, looking so delectable, I will have to forget about taking you out, and just ravish you all day instead."

The desire instantly forming in his expression had her green eyes rounding. She wasn't so sure that was a bad idea.

"Woman!" he groaned as he got up and walked to the door as if it would somehow protect them both. "You were a virgin and you got a serious workout last night. It would do more damage than good for us to go another round. Please, for the sake of my health, too, get showered and dressed before I change my mind."

With those words, he turned and left the suite's bedroom, leaving Haley leaning back against the headboard with a thoughtful smile on her face.

This was what he'd been talking about — this feeling of power, of knowing she was responsible for making his body harden, for making him want her. She was getting a small taste of what it felt like to be a seductress — and she liked it.

Fully awake now and ready for her day out with Crew, she jumped from the bed, letting the sheet drop without feelings of shame as she walked into the bathroom and climbed into the shower. She didn't realize what he was talking about until her hand ran over the outside of her core while she was washing.

She was tender, and now grateful for his consideration. She suspected that walking around would be difficult enough on her.

Panicking for a moment when she realized she was in Crew's suite, she returned to his bedroom, then sighed with relief when she found her newly purchased outfits sitting atop his bed. He thought of everything.

Thankfully, she'd bought some silky panties that wouldn't scrape against her lower regions. With care, she slid them on, and then chose a skirt and blouse.

Haley was happy with what she saw in the mirror. Her new colorful clothes made her feel feminine and appealing. She decided to put on a little makeup, which she'd found after rummaging through the bathroom drawers in search of a washcloth. Who had brought it here and knew that she'd stayed in the owner's suite? It was too mortifying to think about.

She was just finishing placing her hair into a loose bun when Crew joined her.

"You look good enough to lick up and down your entire body. Do you smell just as tasty?" he asked as he pulled her into his arms and lowered his head. As his lips tugged on hers, Haley forgot all about soreness and pushed her body up against his. This was something she could get used to.

With a growl, Crew pulled back and looked deep in her eyes. "Yes. Yes, you do," he said before pulling back and grasping her hands.

"Thanks for having my things here," she said shyly. He must have seen the blush stealing across her cheeks because he answered her earlier question.

"I went to your room and picked up what I thought you might need."

"Thank you, Crew. I don't know if many men would have been so considerate," she said and followed him to the living area.

"Would you like a cup of coffee and a pastry before we go?"

She sat down and happily poured herself a cup, then added cream and sugar before taking a sip. Sighing with pleasure at the much-needed caffeine, she pulled a foot up and hugged her leg while taking small sips and briefly attempting to interpret the clouds in her coffee.

Passing on the pastry so she wouldn't ruin her lunch, she took a moment to study Crew as he conducted a phone call. She didn't understand how the two of them had reached this place so quickly, how she'd had the boldness to make love to him, but she found that she had no regrets. Even if their time together turned out to be short, she knew she'd carry the memories with her for years to come.

Haley had the feeling that getting over a man like Crew wouldn't be an easy task. It didn't matter, though, and it wasn't worth dwelling on. She was living in the here and now, and it was a great place to be. Whatever happened, happened. That was going to be her new motto.

At the very least, she'd walk away with more confidence and knowing she'd been well satisfied and treated well. Her grandmother had always said that all men were only after sex and they didn't care about who they slept with. Even if that was true, she had him in this moment, and that was surely worth something. Besides, she was after sex, too, she thought wickedly.

No one could predict tomorrow with perfect accuracy. All you could do was make a guess, throw in your wager, and hope for the turnout you wanted. And that was what she'd do every day as long as this lasted.

"Are you ready?" he asked as he disconnected his call.

"Yes. Let's see if this café is as good as you think it is."

"Your faith in me is humbling," he said, chortling, and Haley added one more item to her list of things she liked about Crew. He could laugh at himself.

*****

"It may look like a dive, but I'm telling you, Aunt Mae makes the best food I've ever tasted, and I've traveled a lot."

"You haven't lived here very long, have you? I thought you moved here only two years ago."

"I did move here two years ago, but my family owns a home on the other side of the island and we spent at least a couple of weeks a year here. I discovered Aunt Mae's café when I was sixteen, and I've been coming back ever since.

"Well, I hope it's as good as you say because right now I feel like I could take a knife and fork to a grizzly."

Crew stopped and laughed before opening the restaurant door. He was relieved to see her want a decent meal, for too often she just picked at her food. If he'd thought for a moment it was because she was putting on airs or worried about her figure, he'd be disgusted. Women who did that irritated him.

With Haley, he suspected that stress was the biggest problem. If she was worried about something, or frightened, she didn't function right. When she was happy or sated — he'd done a good job with that last night — then she seemed to have a bottomless appetite.

Well, he'd brought her to the right place. Aunt Mae liked to pile on the food. He didn't even bother ordering when he came here. Whatever she decided to bring him was always top notch.

He could see the surprise in Haley's eyes as they walked through the rickety door with tall, lush plants framing it. The building needed a fresh coat of paint and was in desperate need of new furnishings, but no matter how many times he'd offered his help, pleaded with her to accept it, or even tried to force it upon her, Aunt Mae had turned him down flat.

The tables were scarred, but she said that just added to the atmosphere. He knew that one of these days, the rickety chairs were going to leave him with his ass on the floor, but the food was divine and the décor just added to the experience.

Crew and Haley were lucky to find two bar stools open, and they sat down and rested their arms on the worn yet squeaky-clean counter. Behind it was an open window with a behemoth of a man wiping his brow with his forearm as he flipped burgers in the air.

Crew watched Haley eye the colorful posters announcing various menu items; there wasn't a handheld menu in sight. The pies sat in a small display case on the end of the counter, and the oven-baked aromas drifted out to torment them, making Haley's stomach rumble loudly.

"I guess you *are* hungry," he said with a grin as Aunt Mae approached them.

Haley's eyes widened at the stick-thin figure who couldn't reach five feet tall if she were wearing heels. Aunt Mae planted her hands on the counter, then leaned forward and gave Crew a kiss on the cheek before turning suspicious eyes on Haley.

Crew had never brought another woman in here, so he could see the surprise in the woman's eyes and knew she was judging Haley. He wasn't worried. There was something about Haley that drew others to her, and he was sure that by the end of their lunch, Aunt Mae would be trying to coddle her and send her home with a doggie bag loaded with food.

"You haven't visited me in weeks, Crew Storm. What makes you think I'll serve up anything for you to eat?" she pouted, and Crew could see the surprise in Haley's eyes at the deep, husky voice that didn't match her petite face and body. Years of hard booze and cheap cigarettes had given her what was just one of her many charms in Crew's eyes.

"I've been busy getting the new resort running, Aunt Mae. I've noticed you haven't taken up my offer

155

of staying a night and testing out my chefs," he countered, and she blushed.

"I can't stay in your hoity-toity resort. I'd never be able to sleep again in my shabby little room upstairs. I *will* make it over some night to get a free meal. I'm not telling you until it's over, though. I don't want you telling them to fix something special. The best way for me to see if they're good enough to be cooking for you is for them not to know who I am."

Though it wasn't widely known, Aunt Mae had been a top-rated food critic when she was younger. Getting fed up with all the terrible dishes she had to endure, she'd given up her high-paying job and settled down to open her own place nearly thirty years before. The building had been old then, but in better shape.

Hard economic times had made the years rough, but she still had a steady stream of regular customers. One way or another, Crew would make sure she kept the place as long as she liked, even if he had to tie her down while the workers came in and made repairs.

"I wouldn't dream of trying to fool you, Aunt Mae. You are far too wise a woman."

"Don't get cheeky with me, boy! Now, who's this pretty little girl you've brought in?" she asked, turning her full gaze on Haley, who smiled big at her.

"Haley Sutherland. It's nice to meet you."

Crew was shocked by the ease with which Haley spoke to Aunt Mae. A lot of folks were intimidated by her at first, despite her diminutive stature. Haley seemed right at home.

"Well, well. What are you doing out with this hooligan?"

Haley's grin never faltered. "He told me he was going to feed me the best meal I've ever had. I could hardly resist," she said easily as Aunt Mae pulled out a cigarette and lit it, the smoke swirling in the air.

A man from a nearby table grumbled and Aunt Mae's eyes turned to fire as she looked right at him.

"This is my place. If you don't like the atmosphere, you know where the door is," she said pleasantly as she took another drag.

The fellow looked down as he speared a piece of battered fish and continued eating. It appeared he was willing to risk his life with secondhand smoke for the food...*that must be some food*, Haley thought to herself.

"So, Haley, what do you do?"

"Nothing at the moment. I quit my job so I could find a good enough man to teach me how to be the perfect seductress," she replied as if she were speaking of nothing more casual than going to the post office.

Crew's eyes rounded in shock, and he choked on the water he'd just drunk. As he sputtered, he looked from her to Aunt Mae, wondering what his longtime friend was going to say to that remark. After a short pause, she put out her smoke and then laughed. The sound was raspy and a bit wheezy and asthmatic, and he always worried she was going to keel over when she did it.

"I like this one, Crew. I like her a lot, much more than some of those broads I've seen you with in town.

I notice you've been smart enough to never bring one of them in here," she said knowingly.

"I didn't like them enough to give them the treasure of your cooking, Aunt Mae."

"That's a good answer, boy, a good answer," she said. Haley's stomach rumbled again and Aunt Mae turned her eyes back to her. "I'd better feed you before you turn into a skeleton right there in that chair." With that she turned and scribbled something on her notepad before seeing to another customer, who had managed to snag a spot at the end of the counter.

"I like her," Haley commented, making him glow.

It shouldn't have mattered to him what Haley thought of Aunt Mae, but it did. Without realizing it, he'd been testing her. Shyness he could understand, but if she'd turned her nose up at a woman Crew cared about deeply, he wouldn't have wanted to be with her.

"She's a spitfire. Though she's in her sixties, you'd never know it. I think she'll outlive us all," he said as Aunt Mae slapped down a plate between them.

At the look of lust in Haley's eyes over the sizzling cheese, artichoke and spinach appetizer, he fell a bit in love. She'd barely touched his five-course meal, but Aunt Mae's secret menu was making her drool. Haley polished off most of their appetizer, then dug in when her shrimp pasta was placed in front of her.

When she looked at his seafood sandwich with longing, he offered her a bite, then felt himself turning hard at her deep moan of pleasure when she swallowed.

No sex today, he reminded himself. Tomorrow. He'd have plenty of sex with her tomorrow. And somehow he'd better keep her away from his bed for the day if he wanted to keep that promise to himself.

When their plates were cleaned, Haley leaned back with a satisfied grin. "You were right. That's the best meal I think I've ever eaten. I'm going to have to come here over and over while I'm on the island. But right now, I don't think I could eat another bite."

"I don't doubt it," he answered with a chuckle since she'd polished off her meal, then eaten a quarter of his sandwich. It was nice to see her cheeks flushed and a relaxed look in her eyes.

"Here's your dessert, Ms. Haley. This is my special cobbler. Don't even try and guess what's in it; just enjoy the heavenly taste," Aunt Mae said as she placed a warm bowl in front of both of them with sugary berries beneath a perfectly browned crust and vanilla ice cream melting on top.

"I don't know if we can…" Crew started to protest.

"Thank you, Aunt Mae," Haley interrupted as she picked up the spoon and scooped up a large bite, placing it on her tongue. When her eyes rolled back and she sighed in ecstasy, the blood rushed to Crew's groin yet again. This lunch was going to bury him. Had he known eating a meal could be so damned erotic, he would have taken Haley to the corner for a loaded hot dog — extra onions.

When she was halfway through her cobbler, he watched as a piece of berry juice dripped out the corner of her mouth and her tongue emerged to lick it as best as she could. "Let me," he said as he lifted his thumb and rubbed the trace of juice left behind over her chin and then her moist lower lip.

Without thinking — he couldn't stop himself — he leaned forward and sucked on her lip, the taste of berries and ice cream sweet on his tongue. When the tip of her tongue slid across his lip, he had to fight to keep from clinging tightly to her and kissing her the way he wanted to. No, not in front of Aunt Mae. That was for later.

Pulling back, he locked his gaze with hers and filled his eyes with promise. He was going to take her to the furthest reaches of heaven and never let her settle back down on the ground again. The constant stirring inside his body was worth a bit of pain, because he felt alive and ready to conquer the world.

"Crew Storm, that kind of look should be reserved for the bedroom only," Aunt Mae scolded as she set a bag on the counter in front of Haley. Crew couldn't help his wide grin, knowing the woman so well. She couldn't help but feed those she thought needed a little more plumping up.

"What's this?" Haley asked brightly. Crew didn't know how she could even think about wanting more food after the meal she'd eaten, but she eagerly opened the bag and peered in.

"That's a treat for later. You come back and visit me soon, Ms. Haley — and leave Crew at home. I want to have some girl talk."

"Hey..." Crew said with mock hurt.

"I promise I'll be back soon," Haley grinned. Crew had no doubt she'd be there tomorrow if she could get away.

"I gotta get cleaned up now, but I'd better see you both much sooner than your usual two weeks, Crew," she said with a slight glare his way before leaning forward and kissing him on the cheek again, then patting Haley's hand.

Crew pulled out his wallet and slipped two large bills into her tip jar when Aunt Mae wasn't looking, and Haley picked up her prized takeout bag.

The warm breeze blowing outside was perfect for a walk. Strolling back to the resort took them half an hour, but all they did there was leave the bag at the front desk, making sure the staff would have it delivered to Haley's room and refrigerated.

Crew took her on a walk through the touristy area that she hadn't yet visited, and they spent the next couple of hours going in and out of small shops.

When she found a quaint antique store, she rushed inside and started fondling small trinkets and old antiques. An old woodstove with a cast-iron skillet from the eighteen-hundreds then caught Haley's attention; Crew strolled over to a small glass case.

Inside was an old diary, the leather frayed on the cover and edges, but it was open and he could clearly see writing inside. He was certain that the stories it contained would be fascinating. On impulse, he purchased the treasured item and had it wrapped, knowing he'd find a good moment to give it to Haley as a gift. With her dreams of being an archaeologist, she would appreciate the words of an early settler.

When they left, he was also carrying her purchase, an old coffee grinder with a worn wooden box and small cast-iron handle.

"Why would you want that?" He didn't see a use for it.

"Because it's amazing. Imagine the stories that could be told about this box. It's well over a hundred years old, and settlers used it to grind coffee beans in the early morning hours while they heated their water on the stove. Maybe a grandmother rocked her daughter's newborn baby while the mother rested for a few minutes on the other side of a curtain. Doesn't the past fascinate you? Don't you want to know how our ancestors survived harsh winters, the devastation of ruined crops, and enemy attacks?"

Crew honestly had never thought about any of that — he was half asleep during his required history classes — but he didn't want to admit that to her. That he'd ignored where he came from made him feel shallow and self-absorbed.

"We'll have to go tour the one museum here, and more on the mainland." he said.

"Oh yes, that would be so much fun. When I was a teenager, I wanted to own an antique store, but I realized I'd never want to part with any of the items, so I'd never be able to make it. My second dream career would probably be working with documents of the past, or in a museum. It's all just so fascinating. But, if I get my way, I will lead an archaeological dig, discovering an unknown ancient culture. That is the brass ring as far as I'm concerned."

Crew beamed at her and patted his pocket. He'd chosen his gift well, knowing she'd pore through the pages for hours. Paying attention when women spoke was a critical survival skill. He'd learned early that not paying attention could have dire consequences. His sister's wrath when they ignored her had been deadly.

Crew and Haley continued to stroll the streets, but as the sun started to set, his phone rang with a minor emergency at the resort and he had to get back.

"I'll meet you in a couple of hours," he promised before escorting her to the elevator. As the doors shut, he sighed. His day had been far too enjoyable to even think about work right now. But, as his manager came rushing toward him, he put away his personal feelings and focused on his other woman, the resort, and on the man he trusted so well.

Chapter Seventeen

Crew's minor mishap ended up being a couple on the fourth floor who'd left their tub running. By the time it was discovered, the room below it had flooded, too. He'd had to make sure the mess was cleaned up, his inconvenienced guests were transferred to a new hotel, offered full refunds, plus free stays and resort amenities, and the plumber was getting the job fixed quickly. Then, suddenly, it was three in the morning.

Though exhausted, he wanted to go straight to Haley's room, but he didn't want to wake her, so he instead trudged off to his own room, where he took a two-minute shower to wash off the grime from working in the slush, then fell face first into his depressingly empty bed.

Thinking sleep would be hard to come by, he was shocked when he woke up the next morning at eight, two hours later than usual. Not having time for the breakfast with Haley that he'd promised himself the night before, he raced to his office, where he was thrust into a whole host of problems that made him want to pull out his hair.

As the day crept by, he dialed her room when he had a minute, but when he never got an answer, he realized it was time the woman entered the cellular age. Placing a rush order, he had a smart phone brought to the resort and delivered to her room, then tried texting her several times but with no reply.

Where had she disappeared to? He owned neither her nor her time, but as the day wore on, he kept missing her — which was strange in itself. By the time the sun was setting, he found himself wandering through the resort, seeking her company. He was falling in too deeply, he knew, but he had no desire to pull back.

The ever-changing faces of new clientele checking in and others checking out would normally excite him, but nothing seemed to stir his anticipation these days except for a wisp of a blonde who, on paper, was all wrong for him.

None of that mattered.

He wandered into his favorite lounge and found Marlin busy as always with a full crowd circling the bar and filling up the tables as his new pianist lured people in.

The atmosphere was especially animated because tonight was the first day of the Catalina Film Festival, and crowds had flocked to the island in hopes of spotting a favorite Hollywood star. The red carpet was rolled out, limos were traveling through town, and the streets were jammed.

Crew would be lucky to get five minutes alone with Haley over the next five days.

With determination, he took a seat at the bar, determined to get information out of Marlin. His bartender and Haley seemed to be quite chummy, so Crew hoped his loyal employee might know where she was.

As he listened to the clink of glasses and the cheerful voices of his patrons, and waited for Marlin to have a free moment, Crew took out a cigar. He didn't mind waiting — it meant his place of business was busy and a constant stream of cash was flowing in.

"Sorry I took so long, Mr. Storm. We've been swamped all afternoon and into the evening. I don't expect we'll be slowing down any time in the near future," Marlin said as he pulled out a special bottle of single-malt scotch. He grabbed a glass and poured in three fingers of the fine liquor. Marlin pretended to be about to dull the experience with ice cubes, but Crew knew not to fall for that joke anymore.

Crew grabbed the glass and savored the first sip, enjoying the warm burn down his throat. With the night and day he'd had, he could down the entire bottle and still not lose the tension in his shoulders, but no — he wanted to be sober when he found Haley.

"Have you taken any breaks?" Crew asked suspiciously. He knew Marlin would work himself to the bone if he didn't get caught. Crew admired the man's work ethic, but he didn't want his head bartender to get worn out when needed most.

"Why? Are you offering to take over? I think the ladies would enjoy that. You'd get my tip jar filled up real fast," Marlin offered with a cackle, then lit a smoke and took a grateful drag.

Obviously, Marlin hadn't had a break, or even the time to sneak in one of his beloved smokes. Crew had worked the bar before, and he knew the drill well, but tonight he was on a mission and that didn't include warding off drunken socialites who had more money than brains.

"Maybe some other time, but I've been up since last night with only a few hours' sleep. I'm starting to feel it," Crew told him as he blew out a fragrant puff of cigar smoke, which Marlin leaned over to smell.

"Did you notice the two bombshells over in the booth? They've been eyeing you since you walked in. The broads have more plastic on them than a Barbie doll, but man, are they hot! If it wasn't for my old lady, I might give 'em a wink or two. Not that I'm their type." Marlin cackled again at his own brand of wit.

"Yes, I noticed them right off. They're kind of hard to miss in the getups they're…'wearing.' Keep an eye out, and if they get too inebriated, have security escort them upstairs. I don't need anything to happen to the double-D twins," he said with a wink.

"Why don't you just escort them on up yourself? I know how you like the girls with nothing but sex on their mind, and believe me, those women are looking to get laid."

"I think I'll pass, Marlin. They'll find their next victim soon enough." Even as he spoke, one of the girls had begun scanning the room for new prospects since it was obvious Crew wasn't interested. The other one wasn't giving up so easily. He had a bad feeling that if he stayed at the bar too long, she'd work up the energy to approach.

Women like her weren't used to making the first move. They normally had to fend guys off. Well, he wasn't just any guy.

"Yeah, that's what I thought, especially with the way you've been all googly-eyed over Ms. Sutherland," Marlin said as he put out his smoke, then moved down the bar quickly to replace a beer in front of one customer, and a gin and tonic in front of another.

Even if Marlin didn't seem to be paying attention, the man had eyes in the back of his head. He kept the drinks coming so customers never had the opportunity to think about leaving. It was why this lounge was making the most money in the resort, or the island for that matter, by a long shot.

"Speaking of Haley, have you seen her today?" Crew tried to ask casually, but by the triumphant look in Marlin's eyes, he hadn't succeeded in downplaying the way he felt.

That's why women were nothing but trouble, Crew warned himself.

"Yeah, she was in here about an hour ago. Had some soup and crackers, then said something about seeing the show tonight. I bet you're wanting to join her in that nice, dark theater." Marlin mocked him by making a kissing sound.

Seriously, the man was too old to be acting like a horny teenager.

"Maybe," Crew said noncommittally.

He couldn't give *all* his secrets away, after all.

Just as he got up to leave, his phone rang. With a frustrated groan, Crew picked it up, waved goodbye to Marlin, then headed toward his office. Perfect. A little longer until he got to meet up with Haley.

Chapter Eighteen

Crew's luck was out again, for things weren't going at all smoothly at his other lounge. The business there wasn't nearly as good as at Marlin's, and, worse, one of the employees had gotten into a fight with a patron and the manager had to fire the man on the spot. The guy was just lucky Crew hadn't been the one dealing with him.

Crew couldn't stand it when staff got unpleasant with their customers. Even if the customer was in the wrong, there were professional ways of handling it without making his resort look low-class.

Adding insult *and* injury, one of the cocktail waitresses got sick, and his other bartender slipped and sprained an ankle. This was certainly one of those nights in which Murphy's law ruled — anything that could go wrong, did.

So Crew did find himself behind the bar pouring drinks, and he wasn't happy about it. His manager was scrambling to call in replacement staff. This was all part of owning a resort, though. Everyone had to pitch in from time to time, even the owner — or sometimes the owner's family members. Crew would give anything, or almost anything, to have Ashton there with him. Hell, his younger brother had spent several years in Hawaii bartending while taking lessons in surfing, partying and being a jackass playboy. The kid was a pro, but he'd turned things around, thankfully.

Much to Crew's dismay, it didn't take long for the Double-Ds to hunt him down. He watched their eyes light up when they saw him trapped behind the counter. Twin feline grins spread across their faces as they nudged their way up to the bar. Two men eagerly jumped up to give them their stools and, on top of that, paid for their drinks.

Crew couldn't complain. The women had expensive tastes, and their swains' credit cards were racking up some serious income for him. If he ever wanted to sell the resort, the profit margins needed to stay well in the black. So, suppressing his shudders of disgust, he pasted on his most gracious and good-tempered smile as he leaned toward them. Surely a little light flirting couldn't get him into trouble.

"Are you ladies enjoying your stay here at the Catalina Couture?" he asked, keeping his voice low and warm.

"Mmm, well, the night sure has become a lot better now. We were in the film that won the 'Great Communicator' Award," one of them answered.

Crew barely managed to keep his laughter from exploding. He somehow pictured them for a much different type of film than one that would win an award from the Ronald Reagan Presidential Foundation.

"Yes, we can be seen sitting at the bar during a seriously intense scene midway through," the other one piped in eagerly.

"After the filming was over, another director came and spoke to us. He was greatly impressed. We're meeting him next week. Soon, we'll be front and center on the red carpet."

Crew had no doubt which kind of director wanted to meet with them. He was sure that if he himself were interested in triple-X movies, he'd see the two of them front and center *and* wide open.

"That's wonderful. I'm sure I'll see you in the next big Hollywood hit," he said, amazed he was able to keep a straight face. The two of them beamed at him.

"I'm Kadence, and this is my bestie, Roxanne."

He could not care less what their names were. But a businessman's gotta do what a businessman's gotta do. "Lovely names for lovely ladies," he said as he refilled their glasses. *Keep drinking up, girls.* The poor saps they were completely ignoring kept on shelling out cash, and it would probably work in the men's favor.

"You are such a charmer, Crew. What are you doing later tonight?"

The invitation in both their eyes was easily read. He had no doubt that one little nod of his head would have him in bed with the both of them. Nope. He'd never been big on threesomes and he never would be.

"Ah, ladies, you are too much for me to handle. One night with you and I'd never be the same man again," he said as if filled with regret.

"It doesn't need to be just one night, sugar…" Kadence's red-tipped nail trailed down his forearm and Crew was coming to the end of his patience. His flirting wouldn't win him any great-communicator awards.

"Crew, you're free to go do your real job now." Crew turned with relief as his replacement showed up with a smirk on her face. She could read him well, and she knew he wasn't enjoying himself.

The two girls stuck out their bottom lips with a pout. No doubt they'd learned that at acting school for extras.

"It's been a pleasure visiting with you lovely ladies this evening, but duty calls," he said, backing away.

Their disappointed sighs grew fainter and fainter as he fled the bar and made a straight path to the theater. It was time he found Haley. If she'd gone off elsewhere, he was tracking her down one way or another.

Slipping inside the dimly lit room, Crew looked around, wondering how he was going to find Haley in the throng of people crowding the intimate tables arranged strategically around the warm setting.

Like the rest of his resort, the room was filled with a mixture of modern and old-world charm. Tables for two and four were positioned so everyone had a perfect view of the stage, but people weren't knocking into each other.

Along the back wall, where the lights were at their lowest, round bench seats circled tables that were just large enough to hold drinks and appetizers. He saw couples snuggle together while listening to the magical voice of his latest hire, a young woman whom he wouldn't be surprised to hear on the radio quite soon.

Her voice carried the customers off to another world as she sang of lost love and burnt bridges. He wasn't normally a fan of mushy love songs, but with her vocals, it didn't matter what she was singing about. Hand her the Congressional Register and they'd still listen…

Crew finally spotted Haley in a small booth in the back corner. Since she hadn't noticed him yet, he took a moment to appreciate her understated but profound beauty, the dim glow of the lighting leaving half her face in the shadows.

The vocalist had Haley as mesmerized as the rest of his guests; like theirs, her eyes stayed glued to the small stage up front.

Crew was gratified to see his staff moving quietly from table to table, not disturbing the performance in any way, but keeping the guests supplied with drinks and plates of nibbles both warm and cold to keep any loud stomach rumbling at bay.

In the middle of an original song about young heartbreak, Crew slid in next to Haley, finally capturing her gaze and seeing her eyes grow round in pleasure. He knew he was a goner.

In such a ridiculously short amount of time, he was falling head over heels for this woman. She took his breath away, and he found himself wanting to give her the moon and stars. *Oh, good grief.* Shaking his head, he blamed his sappy thoughts on the lyrics and voice bewitching the room. Who wouldn't think of happily-ever-afters here? He'd created the room with just that in mind — though not for himself.

Trying to gain back the breath that seemed to have left his chest, Crew leaned closer and took Haley's lips, running his tongue along the soft lines of her lush mouth until she lifted her hands up and grasped his neck, deepening the kiss as if their recent time apart had been painful for her, too.

Before their embrace got too heated for public consumption, he reluctantly pulled back and looked into her glowing eyes. The light from the soft wall sconces and dripping chandeliers made them almost translucent. Losing himself in them was exactly what he wanted to do.

"It's good to see you," he whispered as he nuzzled her neck.

"I will spend the day apart from you any time if I get another kiss like that," she said huskily. He wanted to take her from the room right then and show her just how much he'd missed her.

"Good evening, Mr. Storm. Shall I get you your usual?"

With a sigh, Crew leaned back and nodded at his waitress. "Add spinach dip and fresh baked chips, and have Joey throw in a bowl of soup." He was starving. Normally, only appetizers were served in the theater, but that didn't apply to him.

"Oooh, I'll have the same, but can I have some bread, too?" Haley piped in.

His waitress nodded and hurried away.

"You haven't eaten yet?" he asked.

"No. I was running around town today and forgot. Then, I was so entranced by the show, food was the farthest thing from my mind. Now that you brought it up, though, I can't think of anything else."

"We can leave and I will take you to a real dinner. Or, better yet, we can go to my room and order room service. I have a sudden desire for strawberries and champagne, preferably eaten off your skin."

Haley's eyes shone as she seriously considered his suggestion. One word, and he'd have gladly left the table and hauled her away.

"No. It would be rude to walk out on her performance. She's doing a beautiful job. We'll have the soup as an hors d'oeuvre, then the strawberries for dessert," she promised.

Crew's body instantly hardened at her bold words. Where was the shy yet determined woman he'd first met? It seemed she was slowly being replaced by this more confident, alluring female, and he could barely keep his hands off her.

Though the vocalist's performance remained flawless, Crew kept glancing at his watch. His overheated body had been pressed against hers for only one night, and now he needed a repeat performance.

The food came and it helped to get the edge off at least one of his hungers, but did nothing for the insatiable need still tearing at his insides. When the final song ended, Crew clapped loudly, a little for his singer, and a lot because now he could get Haley alone.

"Let's go," he said urgently; he jumped up and held out a hand.

"Aren't you eager!" She smiled and let him assist her from the intimate booth.

"You can't imagine," he groaned as he began leading her toward the doors.

"I know you want to get up there immediately, Crew, but I'm so warm right now. Would you mind taking a small stroll outside with me first?"

Haley must secretly hate him and want him to expire from sexual frustration, he decided. Yet unable to deny her request, he slapped down the monster clawing to be freed from inside of him, and led her through the lobby and out the back doors, moving quickly to the beach.

This would be the fastest stroll he'd ever taken — not that he was a man who normally took strolls. He was either running or sleeping; there didn't seem to be a middle ground with him.

"Amari is a beautiful singer. I could listen to her all night," Haley said. When they reached the edge of

177

the water, she slipped off her shoes and let the waves splash over her toes. He was forced to retreat a step back or ruin his favorite leather loafers.

"Yes, I was lucky to find her before a record label picks her up. It won't take long — she's amazingly talented. I have a contract for eight weeks, though, so this may very well be her last personal gig before she records something and hits it big."

He didn't want to speak about his headliner act. He wanted to talk about the two of them, but he could see that Haley was avoiding the topic for some reason. Alarm bells rang in his mind, and in his groin. If he didn't take her tonight, he would need to take one heck of a long swim in the cool water currently caressing her feet — something he'd rather be doing himself.

"I grew up less than a hundred miles from the ocean, but still I never made it there until a couple of years ago. How sad is that? I wonder how many people have similar stories to tell. There is just so much beauty in this world, and most of us don't even see one percent of it. Someday, I'll travel the entire world and look in the most ancient of museums and touch as many of the Wonders of the World — ancient, medieval and modern — as I can. I am feeling a need to roam now, thinking I may just leave school for a while and travel…"

Her dreamy sigh told him she would do that, but he didn't want her to leave without him. When people's dreams were big enough and their will strong enough, they could make anything happen. He'd seen it countless times before. It was when people gave up that their life dwindled to nothing. What was the point of existing in this world if you didn't really live your life to its fullest potential?

To hell with the distance between them. Crew threw off his shoes and socks in seconds and stepped in the water with her. The bottom of his custom slacks were instantly soaked, but he didn't care.

Maybe a part of her was trying to keep him at a distance, but he didn't want that and if she was honest, she didn't want it either. She was just protecting herself, reverting to her old habits. He could feel her withdrawal in the melancholy mood she was in. He didn't know what had brought it on, but he was determined to find out, and refused to allow her to slip away.

"Nothing is as beautiful as you, and I can guarantee you that anywhere you want to go can happen," he said, his hand coming up to caress her cheek. Though it might sound a bit cheesy — par for the course that evening — he truly felt those words as he looked into her eyes.

She took his breath away far more than any sunset ever had, than any of the Wonders he'd been lucky enough to visit. She was a vision, and she was his for now.

Crew waited, his fingers rubbing her delicate skin, but he wanted her to choose the kiss, he wanted her to be in control. She needed that, and then he wouldn't feel the guilt of knowing he'd coerced her into it. He needed her to choose him.

Yes, he could seduce her — easily. But, he wanted more than the night before, more than tonight.

He wanted to be with her without thought of an end in sight.

Slowly, she relented; her hands reached into his hair and she pulled his mouth to hers, her tongue demanding entrance. Just having him hold her was enough to lift the unseen burden she was carrying on her shoulders. She knew he was strong enough to carry it for her if only she could bring herself to let him.

He nearly lost his balance in the gently lapping ocean waves as his raw hunger awakened with a vicious groan. Fire licked at his gut, and no matter how she touched him, he hungered for more, his body demanding her total compliance.

Letting her lead him for a few more moments, Crew knew his control wouldn't last much longer, so he began walking them backward out of the cool water.

"Come to my room." She was ready — so was he. He didn't want to start their lovemaking in the sand. He hadn't cleared it with his staff to leave them alone, and it would kill him to be interrupted once he started. He was too damned hungry for her.

She didn't speak, but the slight nod of her head was better than love songs to his ears. Grasping her hand, he led her back up the beach and through the French doors, making a beeline for the elevator.

He looked straight ahead, unwilling to risk even eye contact with anyone. This time, he didn't care if the place caught fire. He wasn't going to be called away from her side.

Doing something he hadn't done once in the last two years, Crew pulled out his cell phone as they entered the elevator and pushed the power button. He felt total victory as the small picture on the screen disappeared and his main means of contact with his staff was terminated.

A small lamp was burning in his room, just enough light so they wouldn't bump into the furniture, but not enough to ruin the moment. Hesitating long enough only to unplug the resort phone, too, he backed her toward his bedroom.

Her body shook as he pushed her gently but firmly, causing her to land with a satisfying bounce on his soft comforter. Tonight was going to be so much more magical than her first time. He now knew how innocent she was, so he would take his time and make her think of no other man but him ever again. He would end any and all thoughts she had of leaving him behind.

Chapter Nineteen

Haley so wanted to cover herself, but she resisted the urge as she lay naked before him. Crew obviously desired her — there was no hiding that he'd been ready to take her the moment they touched — and they couldn't make love while all her clothes were on. But the supreme self-consciousness she'd lived with for so many years didn't disappear overnight. He didn't give her time to dwell on it, though.

She sighed in pleasure as Crew's hands slid across her torso, skimming over her waist, then moving higher and gliding across the sides of her breasts. He used just his fingertips to excite her skin, making her heart pound and her breathing grow ragged. He knew how to give pleasure, and luckily, she was the sole focus of his desire.

Accepting that this was where she wanted to be, this was where she'd always longed to be, took away the burden of guilt that her grandparents had instilled in her. She'd never truly known pleasure before lying in Crew's arms, and she feared she'd never know it again once this affair ran cold.

Chasing away these negative thoughts, she embraced the woman within her and greedily took everything he was willing to give as his mouth began trailing across her jaw, just grazing the edges of her lips as his sweet breath warmed her face. It was both torment and pleasure, and she was already beginning to fly.

When his tongue began lazily stroking the edges of her lips, she tried to pull him to her, tried to fuse their mouths together, needing the torment to end, but he had other ideas. He was obviously in no hurry.

Considering the pace at which they were moving, they'd probably still be making love when the early morning sun rose high in the sky. Oh, well. There could be worse things. Relaxing into the gentle caress he offered, she tightened when he began nibbling her bottom lip, applying gentle pressure as he threw his shirt off, then lay across her body.

"Sex is all about the touch, taste and smell. Trust me," he said.

She found her hands raised above her head and then felt that she couldn't move them. What was this? She struggled against his makeshift bonds as her eyes opened.

"Crew?" she whimpered.

"Tell me to stop if at any moment you're not feeling pleasure," he said and kissed each of her

183

eyelids before slipping his tie across her eyes and making the room go dark.

"I don't think I like this," she whispered as his hand trailed between her breasts and down the flat of her stomach.

"Do you want me to stop?"

When Haley was silent, he continued to speak. "I didn't think so. This is your next lesson — on touch. If you want a man to desire you, then you need to know what you like, Haley. You need to tune out the world around you and focus only on *your* body and *your* needs," he said before his mouth captured her taut nipple and sucked it deep within.

"Do you like this?" he asked as he paused before moving to her other breast and giving her other peaked nipple equal attention.

"Yes," she sighed as her back arched.

"And, this?" he asked as he moved lower to skim over her stomach with his mouth.

"Yes." Moaning as his hands slid up her thighs, she spread them wide.

"Tell me what you like."

She paused, feeling her face grow warm. How could she do that? She didn't know what she liked — she just knew that everywhere he touched sent fire through her veins.

"If you don't tell me what you like, don't tell me how to touch you, then I won't know. Remember to *feel* the pleasure, think about where it begins and branches out. Think about what will drive you over the edge."

His seductive words were mesmerizing her, and her muscles went slack as his hands slid up and down her thighs, making flames of heat shoot through every inch of her body.

When Crew's mouth moved back up her torso, she was frustrated and disappointed that he hadn't continued south and given her the pleasure he had the last time. She couldn't tell him that, though, could she?

As his lips brushed across hers, teasing them into opening, she gratefully took his tongue inside her mouth, entwining it with her own. Burning need raged deep with her, and she now knew that he was right — being blind and unable to move her hands electrified her other senses, made them spring to life with new vigor and intensity.

Focusing on every touch of his hands, body and mouth made her tremble in his arms as she eagerly awaited his next move.

"Where do you want me to touch you?" he asked as he moved over, now pressing the warmth of his chest against her side and swirling his tongue around her ear.

"Everywhere," she gasped.

"That's not good enough, Haley. Tell me where you burn, where you want me to relieve the ache," he whispered into her ear, causing tremors to race through her.

After a pause, she threw away her embarrassment. "My breasts," she gasped, her nipples hard and aching, elongating as her body arched beautifully

185

toward him, needing his soothing tongue to quench the burning.

He swiftly obliged, his tongue laving one nipple until it glistened, then the next, before latching onto each of them in turn. He circled his tongue over her pink areola, then gently nipped the hardened peak, before repeating on the other side. It relieved the ache there, but made her stomach tremble with need.

He didn't move, forcing her to try to twist in his arms. If she'd had her hands free, she would have pushed his head down, moved him where she now needed his mouth so desperately. Knowing that he wouldn't go elsewhere until she asked him filled her with frustration, and yet power, too. She was in control here with nothing but her words.

"Lower," she gasped as he sucked her nipple harder.

Crew obliged, running his tongue along her stomach, trailing light kisses up and down her torso and sides. He traced every inch of her skin there, stoking her heat to white hot, making need layer on top of need until she felt she would explode.

"Lower," she called breathlessly, and he moved to her thighs, his tongue slipping along the inside of her legs, licking the sensitive skin just outside her core. He sucked on her quivering flesh, but he still wouldn't give her what she truly wanted.

The throbbing inside her seemed to be taking on a life of its own. Could she possibly blow up if he didn't relieve the ever-mounting pressure? She was certain that could happen. If a boiler built up this much steam without someone pulling the valve and letting it release, there would be a giant crater in the ground. She just had to do something, say something, now.

"Lick me, Crew, please," she begged. His tongue ran along her thighs. "No! Take my heat; make me come in your mouth!" she demanded, tossing her head from side to side.

"Oh, my…" she screamed when his lips clamped down on her swollen core. The textured tip of his tongue ran in circles around her moist flesh, and she felt the buildup of pressure go into the red zone.

"Yes, Crew, yes!" she praised. This was the spot. This was where she wanted, *needed* his masterful technique now.

With a few more exquisite passes from his tongue, Haley exploded into a paradise all her own. There was no gentle falling. This was a detonation of light and sound, of pure adrenaline almost to the point of pain, a wonderful, mind-blowing pain. Never had she imagined feeling such intensity.

She shook as his hand moved below her, gripping her quivering backside as he ran his tongue across her flexing skin a couple of times more. When he released her, she melted into the bed, her eyes rolling into the back of her head behind the silk tie still secured there.

When she felt his hands at her arms, she jumped, her flesh feeling like one big erogenous zone. She couldn't possibly do anything else.

All of a sudden, she was free. Her arms fell limp to the bed, and she felt his gentle fingers rubbing over them, making the blood run through their length.

Next, the tie came off and she squinted at him in the dim light as she forced her eyes open.

"That was magnificent," she told him and smiled lazily into his strained face.

"It's about to reach a whole new level, Haley. I've only begun."

"Ooh," she said in a whoosh of breath. The thought of more should have terrified her, but a stirring began in the pit of her stomach, where her body still trembled from the powerful release he'd just given her.

"What do you want now?"

Her eyes widened. She was still in control, able to demand anything she wanted from him. As she looked down his perfect body, she knew she wanted only one thing.

"You. Deep inside me."

Crew seemed to speak another language his words were so inarticulate before he immediately sheathed himself and then lay on top of her. Thinking he would slam inside without preliminaries, she tensed, waiting for the initial pain again.

When he lubricated her moistness with the tip of his erection and slowly inched in, she felt herself relax, enjoying the stretching of her skin, as inch by beautiful inch he filled her.

"Deeper," she called, "faster." She was done with slow and steady. As her stomach tensed with a renewed need, she wanted speed and friction — she wanted the burning release she'd received only from him.

"Like this...?" he asked seductively as he pushed forward, burying himself deep inside her.

"Yes, Crew. Always like this, always! Take me," she demanded as her legs wrapped around him. She didn't know who she was anymore, but his presence was giving life to an insatiable monster, a man-eater, even, and she hoped the creature never retreated.

"Open your eyes, Haley. I want to see the pleasure explode in them when I slam against your body."

She did as he asked, looking deep inside his eyes as he began moving his hips, bringing her closer and closer to the peak again. She could do this night and day and still it wouldn't make up for the years she'd lost without it.

How could she somehow experience something so magical and then never do it again? She didn't think she could ever let him leave the bed after this night.

Sounds of pleasure and slick coupling filled the air, heightening her craving for more. Her mind had only one thought — how to find the way to another delicious orgasm. As he tightened against her and called out her name, she fell with him, lost in an abyss of darkness, her body turned to liquid and sated to the fullest.

As he pulled from her, she turned, snuggling down deep, deciding she'd never leave the safe softness of his bed again.

His hand stroked along her side, and Haley smiled, loving his touch, completely content in this perfect moment.

"Round three, beautiful. We're not done yet," he whispered, making goose bumps appear on her skin.

He had to be kidding. She was spent. Yes, she'd just told herself that she never wanted this to stop, but surely there were limits to human sensation. There was no possible way she could do that all over again. Her nervous system just couldn't take it.

Haley ignored his words, but as Crew continued to stroke her skin, unbelievably, her body awakened again, and she found herself turning toward him.

It was a couple of hours more before, despite a touch of soreness, she found the sweet pleasure of oblivion. Her last thought before she descended into sleep was that the pain was well worth that incredible night of lovemaking.

Chapter Twenty

Waking up with the morning sun streaming through Crew's window, Haley stretched her arms and connected with the firm muscles of Crew's naked chest.

Deliciousness.

For just a moment, she practically purred, but reality quickly dropped down with a thud. She didn't know the rules of a game such as this. Was she supposed to slip quietly out the door? When she'd slept over before, he'd woken her up and had her out the door so fast, she didn't have time to think about any of those things.

Crew Storm could have any woman he wanted, and he had many of them figuratively notched on his impressive bedpost. She knew she was a novelty item, the virgin who'd asked him to be her teacher.

Thinking back, she'd been quite naïve and unaware of what she'd been asking.

Teach her he had, though. She could feel confidence flowing through her. Though it wouldn't be easy, or even possible, to be an entirely new person, at least she felt attractive, and she knew she didn't belong in a corner. The problem was that she wanted to belong by his side.

Should she play it cool? Act as if this were no big deal? He was well aware that it wasn't something she did all the time, but he seemed to prefer confident socialites — that's what she'd read, anyway — so should she try and mold herself into one of them to stay at his side a while longer?

No.

Even if that was what he wanted, she couldn't pretend to be one of those shallow women. She was just Haley Sutherland, a girl who'd missed out on life while the rest of the world continued spinning rapidly around her. *I am what I am.*

Just as she was deciding it was time to get up and sneak off to her room and wait for his next move, his arm snaked out and pulled her tightly against his side.

"Good morning, my little siren. I hope you slept well," he mumbled against her neck, making all sorts of tingles dance in her stomach.

"Very well, thank you."

"I could use a large cup of coffee, and a gigantic breakfast. I feel like I ran a marathon," he said with a laugh.

His positive mood was a good thing. She'd just take her cue from him.

"The coffee sounds wonderful, but I need a hot shower first," she said as she stretched her legs out and felt the soreness in her thighs. Feeling it made a grin spread across her face. She'd take her workouts beneath him any day over on top of a treadmill.

"Scratch what I said before. I'll join you — coffee can wait." His mouth was doing wicked things to her body, but she couldn't go there again so soon. Maybe after a day of rest...

"I think I'll take the shower alone for the sake of my sore...muscles," she replied, giggling.

"Ah, you have no imagination," he said with a wolfish grin, but his grasp loosened as he sat up in bed, then gently gripped her beneath the arms to help her up, slinging one of his arms around her back so she was still snuggled against him.

The feel of his hand massaging her back had her melting into him. His touch could turn her on fire, or soothe away her fears. A very talented man.

Her heart suffered a sudden pang of alarm while he held her in his arms. Many times she'd see lovers embracing in a park, or cozying up together at the movies. She'd envied their obvious ease in each other's company. Now that she was getting a taste of it, she feared having to give it up.

Idly, her fingers stroked along his chest, memorizing the map of his toned muscles. She could sit like this the rest of the day and feel that there was no better thing to do in the world. Who needed to get up and work when they had a strong man to hold them in his arms all day, instead?

"I'm loving just holding you, Haley, but my body has other ideas. I don't know how, but it does. If you don't run away to the shower soon, I can't be held responsible for my actions," he warned with a playful nip on her shoulder.

The heck with being sore. It was worth it to have him pressed against her. As if he could read her thoughts, he gently shifted her away and rose from the bed with a pained but resolute expression across his beautiful features.

As he turned, her eyes were glued to his magnificent backside while he walked toward his discarded clothes and bent over. The muscles flexing in his legs were a sight to behold. She'd never been interested in painting, but as the early morning sun streamed down on his rock-hard body, she suddenly had a desire for a paintbrush and canvas. Perfection such as his should be recorded for all time.

Inspiration hit when she saw her new cell phone on the nightstand. With a quick lunge, she snatched it up and focused on his bare behind, then snapped a couple of shots. He turned incredulous eyes on her when he heard the click.

"All right, woman, get your shower. I'll have breakfast waiting when you come out," he said, glaring at her small black device before coming back over and giving her a lingering kiss. A low growl escaped his throat, but he turned and walked from the room.

Haley savored the moment, closing her eyes, leaning her head back, and inhaling deeply. She allowed herself to just soak it all in and think of nothing other than the fast rhythmic tempo of her heart. He was a heartbreaker — she had no doubt about that — but she was just too satisfied, too relaxed to care about that right now.

Finally getting up, she showered quickly, eager for that cup of coffee. Finding his oversized robe, she wrapped it around her body, then followed her nose to the smell of rich brewed espresso.

Crew was sitting at the table reading the paper while he sipped on a steaming mug, and she joined him, preparing her cup before grabbing a warm cinnamon roll and taking a bite, sighing as the fresh cinnamon, sugar and melted butter dripped on her tongue.

"Let's move your things in," he said, not looking up from his newspaper.

Haley's eyes bolted up, her bite turning to sawdust in her mouth. Was he speaking to her?

"Excuse me?" she managed to mumble after a strained pause.

"I want you to move out of your room and come stay with me," he replied as he put the paper down, his eyes gazing steadily back at her.

How did she reply to this? She hadn't known him long enough to stay in his suite. That was insane, wasn't it?

"I, ah, don't think that would be wise," she replied, automatically lifting her cup and taking a fortifying sip of her coffee, hoping the caffeine would clear the cobwebs from her brain.

"I plan on spending every night with you anyway, so wouldn't it be much easier to just have your items here? This is a resort, Haley. It's not like I'm asking you to give up your house," he said as if he were making the most logical statement ever.

"Well, I just like to have my space," she murmured.

He paused for a moment, looking at her quizzically. "Where do you live, anyway?"

It was a perfectly rational question, but she'd seem pathetic if she told him the truth. Dread filled her that he might realize she was indeed pitiful, and then end what they had barely even started.

"It doesn't matter. I think we're fine the way we are. So, any good articles in your paper?" Maybe she could sidetrack him with a change of subject.

Her ploy didn't work.

"Come on, Haley. Give me something," he said, then leaned across the table and grasped her free hand. She took another sip of coffee, scalding her tongue slightly.

"I live in Seattle in an apartment," she murmured, her voice barely above a whisper.

"That's not so bad. Why are you hesitant to tell me?"

"I don't know. I just don't like to give out too much information about myself. I guess it's from the years of having to be self-reliant. It's difficult for me to share…" she trailed off.

Crew looked at her strangely, just as she'd expected him to. She was hard to understand. Heck, she couldn't really understand herself. How was she supposed to explain it to him?

"Did you have any other family you could turn to? I know your grandparents should have been drawn and quartered for the way they treated you, but was there anyone else in your life at all?"

This was a subject that Haley absolutely hated speaking about. No. She hadn't had anyone in her life but the servants at her grandparents' place, and even those relationships had faltered over the years. She hated dwelling on how alone she truly was. She'd fantasized about being part of a large, loving family, but had given up on that dream years before. She didn't want him to fully comprehend how messed up her life was. This sharing of her past and present wasn't what she'd signed on for.

"I had some rough years with my grandparents, as you know. I have fought against all the doubts they instilled in me since I got away from that 'home,' but I tend to psych myself out about it all too often. Going to school has really helped, but at the end of the day when I look in the mirror, I still see this person whom nobody wanted. I promise it's getting better, but I've just had to do whatever it takes to make it day by day. If I think too far ahead, I get overwhelmed, and that's when I find myself start sinking within myself." She held her breath, waiting for him to roll his eyes and give up on her. She was too crazy for a man like Crew, who had it all together.

Now he was going to know she was too much effort, and she'd never get the privilege of sleeping in his arms again. The thought was horribly depressing.

Crew's gaze didn't shift as he brought his cup up and took a sip.

"All the more reason for you to move in with me. You need to have someone take care of you. We'll go pack your things after breakfast." Treating the matter as closed, he set down the mug, picked his paper back up and started reading again.

Haley ran her hands through her hair and stared at the back of his newspaper. Was he the one who was insane? Why wasn't he trying to delve deeper, get into her head, or just send her packing? If *she* knew she wasn't completely together, why couldn't *he* see it?

Yet wasn't she overanalyzing this, and trying to seek out serpents in her temporary paradise? It wasn't as if she couldn't just move back out again when their relationship, or whatever this was called, ran its course. He hadn't mentioned anything about her two-week vacation. Did he want her to stay longer? Doubtful.

It might be best to avoid reminding him that she was only here because she'd won a raffle. If she brought that up right now, he might snap out of this spell he seemed to be under and tell her that he'd personally pack her bags and get her to the airport to send her off. The thought of leaving him in a couple of days turned her stomach inside out.

With a sigh, she looked at her breakfast, the once delicious cinnamon roll now turning her stomach. There seemed no need to respond to Crew anymore, since he'd already made up his mind, and to tell the truth, she wanted to sleep by his side each night. At least for a while, she could pretend this was a normal relationship, and that this incredible man cherished her. A little fantasy would help her sleep on those nights when loneliness was eating her alive.

Making up her mind, she pushed away her plate and took small sips from her cup while she tried to convince herself that it was OK to seek enjoyment from life. It was OK to not worry about what tomorrow would bring. She'd see this through to the natural end, and she'd grow as a person. That was all she could ask of herself and Crew.

Chapter Twenty-One

A few days later, Haley felt obliged to tell Crew that her time was up. Her train ticket was for the next day, and though she didn't want to leave, she needed to get back to the real world. She'd always believed that the word *heartache* was a metaphor, but there was no denying the physical pain in her chest as she stood in the bathroom and practiced her goodbye speech.

Would he ever think of her again? In time, would she get over him? She and Crew had been together only two weeks, but they were two glorious weeks, and she knew she'd never be the same.

That was all thanks to him, and to his wonderful lessons. Her gloom didn't prevent a contented grin from spreading across her features when she thought of the magic he'd created within her. She now knew it wasn't a sin to enjoy sex; it wasn't a crime to feel like a woman.

Her grandparents had been so wrong in so many ways, and she wished they were still alive so she could confront them with their cruelty. Was it always wrong to think ill of the dead? They'd tried their hardest to destroy her, and they'd almost succeeded, so she didn't think so in this case. As long as she didn't descend into anger and bitterness, they wouldn't control her from beyond the grave.

It was amazing how much could change within a person in such a short amount of time. She knew she had a long way to go before she'd be the person she wanted to be, but because of Crew, she was much closer than she'd ever been.

Taking a soothing breath, she gripped the doorknob and emerged from the warm bathroom. She could hear the crinkling of the paper as Crew turned the page. After closing her eyes for a moment to imprint everything to her memory, she moved forward.

No matter what, she wouldn't cry. Why make him feel guilty about her pain? Everything he'd ever done was meant to help her feel better about herself.

He mumbled a good morning as she sat and poured herself a cup of coffee, and grabbed a chocolate croissant. With the churning in her stomach, she doubted she'd be able to eat, but it was such a habit now to sit at this small table while he read the paper and she nibbled on the goodies before her while downing a couple of cups of espresso.

"I was thinking of playing hooky today, Haley, and taking you out to see the Catalina Island Conservancy so you can see the bison. You told me last week that you wanted to do some exploring."

Crew set down the paper to focus all of his attention on her. Normally, he finished reading first, then gave her his undivided attention. On the morning she had to tell him goodbye, his extra attention hurt even more. Could the man get any more perfect? Was he really as flawless as she'd made him in her mind, or was she just placing him on a pedestal?

There was no need to drag this out, so she plastered a fake smile on her face. "I really need to pack today. My train leaves early tomorrow," she said, proud she'd been able to say the words without trembling.

Crew froze and his face lost all expression; his eyes bored into hers. After a few moments, he finally set his cup down.

"I don't want you to leave." It was simple and to the point and her heart began to swell in joy…*but wait. Maybe he's just saying that.*

"I know, Crew. I'm having a wonderful time here, too, but the package I won was for only two weeks, and my time is up…" she said, her voice starting to crack just the slightest bit.

"Screw the contest. Are you happy being here with me?"

"Of course I am," she replied with exasperation. It wasn't about her happiness; it was about her time being up.

202

"Do you have a job to get back to?" She shook her head *no*. She'd quit to come on this trip.

"Aren't you on break from school right now?" Again, he was correct, so she nodded.

"But, Crew —"

"I don't see any reason for you to leave. I want you to stay. You want to be here, and you have no obligations calling you back to Seattle right now. Let's cancel your return and go see the bison."

She wanted that so badly, but...

"Look, Haley. Let's not make this complicated, OK? We like each other. It's still new and exciting, and I'm not asking you for forever, here. I'm asking you to give me a chance. Let's have fun together, light the sheets on fire, and not throw this out the window just because of semantics."

He rose from his chair and came around to her, kneeling in front of her and caressing her thighs. She couldn't think when he touched her like this. She knew she should protest, just a little, but she'd suddenly forgotten why. And she wanted to be with him, wanted to feel his touch, sleep in his bed, hear his words of encouragement. She wanted to continue having the feelings of love and affection she felt while in his arms — whether hot and heavy in the bedroom or just cuddling on the beach. Was she asking for too much?

Really, what would it hurt for her to stay another week or two? It wouldn't alter her life in the least. It may even make her that much stronger in the end.

"I don't know..." she hedged, trying not to be rash.

As if he'd already won, Crew smiled before standing up and pulling her into his arms. "Let me convince you, then," he said as he lifted her up and carried her toward the bedroom.

"I need to think, Crew," she whispered as he set her on the bed.

"No you don't. Obviously you get poor ideas in your head when you try to reason out what the right choice is. Let me remind you of why you can't leave," he replied as he parted her robe and began nibbling on her neck.

"Ohh," she moaned, trying to focus but quickly losing the battle. The man did crazy things to her crazier mind, and that was fine by her.

As he began moving his head down her body, she gave up any ideas of going "home." Her heart was right here — at least for the moment.

They didn't make it out to see the bison…

*****

Haley kept checking the calendar, counting the days, and shaking her head in disbelief. August had hit and she was still with Crew.

Marlin had told her that Crew was choosy about his women, that the scandals about him in the papers were made-up lies. Still, even Aunt Mae was surprised by the length of time that she and Crew had been together. He wasn't known for long relationships. Should Haley still be afraid? He'd said nothing of a more permanent relationship, but he also didn't seem in the least bit of a hurry for her to go.

She had to make a decision about whether to get back to the real world or not, though. School started in a month. She needed to choose that or travel…

Most mind-boggling of all was that he continued his *lessons* with her. She found small trinkets on the nightstand, flowers on the bathroom counter, her favorite coffee waiting for her when she woke up after he'd had to rush out and miss their breakfast together.

The greatest present she'd received had been the day he'd taken her on his private boat to a secluded beach on the island. They'd had a picnic, and he presented her with a map he'd had made, then walked with her as she went on a treasure hunt.

At the end of the hunt, she'd found an antique chest, and inside had been a beautiful old journal, antique sterling silver cup and hankie from the eighteen-hundreds. She'd treasure those items forever. Already, she'd spent countless hours poring over the words of the journal, tears falling as she read about the heartbreak of the woman writing in it when she'd lost her infant child.

In this new age, it was hard to imagine that common ailments that we simply shrug off today could lead to death back then. Still, even though it broke her heart to read the words of this brave woman, she couldn't put the gift down, knowing she'd treasure it forever.

Twice, Crew had had to leave for a couple of days, and when he came back, he hadn't been empty-handed, bringing her a glorious string of sapphires and gold that she refused to take off, and an anklet that was their own personal joke.

He told her that if it had been the days of old, he'd have had her chained to his bed, where he could feast upon her day or night. She replied that she would be an open buffet for him any time he liked, no chains required. Still, each time she looked at the little lock on her ankle, she felt herself grow warm as she imagined what new adventure he'd take her on that night.

The sex was otherworldly. Sometimes it was hot and passionate, with clothing shredded and flying in their passionate frenzy to fuse with each other. At other times, it was slow and sweet. He'd lick her all over while his hands caressed her heated skin. No matter how they made love, the crashing conclusion was always the same — explosions and fireworks and an afterglow that bonded her closer to him.

But it couldn't last. Haley knew that good things never did. Once a servant of her grandparents had given her a Pound Purrie, an adoptable "down on her luck" kitty found in a charity thrift shop. She'd loved that ratty, stained stuffed animal with all her starved soul. Then one day it just disappeared. OK, Crew couldn't be likened to her grandparents. He was kind and attentive, but he was simply too wonderful, too good for her. The other shoe was poised to drop. After all, the Catalina Couture Resort was for sale, and there was a very interested buyer.

But she had to be grateful. "Take this day as if it's your last, Haley. Live, love, laugh," she told her reflection in the mirror. To live truly happy for even a short time was so much better than to walk through life as an empty shell.

There was no time to dwell on the future. She didn't know what it would hold. All she knew for sure was that for today she was a happy person — carefree and with a terrific man. Well, she would be carefree and happy if she'd quit stressing over every little thing for ten seconds.

Crew had business meetings all day long, so she planned to go shopping. The island wasn't a place for good bargains — for that, you needed to go to the mainland — but laziness was seeping through her bones. She'd stroll the beaches and check out some of the gift shops here on the island, part of a private tour to take it all in before she moved back home.

One thing she knew for sure was that her life was forever changed. She wouldn't hide in the corner anymore, and she wouldn't be afraid to go after what she wanted. Once she'd left Catalina Island behind, she would move forward, finish her degree and go on that dig someday. She wasn't going to give up on herself ever again. Hey, maybe she'd even get a cute little house, or a nice apartment with access to a swimming pool.

Wherever she ended up, she was going to be a grown-up and make adult decisions. There was no need to keep being fearful she was this person her grandparents had convinced her she was — an abomination that no one wanted.

Now that she'd had a small taste of security and love, she wanted it on a more permanent basis. Her grandparents' taunts were a thing of the past; she wouldn't let those people haunt her from the grave.

Leaving the room with a smile on her face, and a future filled with endless opportunities, Haley pushed aside her fears of no tomorrow with Crew as she entered the lobby, then decided to go out the back door and walk to town by way of the beach. The breeze was a bit warm, but the waves were calling to her.

Stepping onto the patio, she looked to the right and froze. Crew was standing in the center of a group of people with big smiles on their faces as a petite redhead had her arms wrapped tightly around him.

With Haley's jaw gaping open, she watched as the woman kissed him loudly on the cheek and then told him how much she'd missed him and civilized life. With a burst of laughter, Crew lifted her from the ground and spun her in a circle.

After the initial shock, fire ran through Haley's veins, and she fought the urge to rush forward and rip the girl's hair out. How dare he humiliate her like this! No, she and Crew were not committed, there were no promises of forever, but he could have at least had the decency to end it with her before moving on to his next conquest.

She'd certainly been giving him enough sex to appease ten men, and yet he'd still felt a need to cheat on her. She wanted to destroy both of them, then kick him so hard he'd never be able to please another woman.

Before she could screech and act on her impulse, she took a fortifying breath and thought back to all the lessons he'd taught her on how to be more confident, how to make a man desire her so much, he couldn't see straight.

Squaring her shoulders, she strode into the small alcove, watching as Crew's eyes lifted and met hers. The jerk didn't even have the decency to look ashamed that he'd been so blatantly caught out.

"I see your morning meetings are going well. It seems you've even made your next major acquisition," she spat. She was trying to control her voice, but the venom running wild in her blood seeped through her words.

His smile fell away, replaced by a look of surprise. The cheating creep hadn't even removed his arm from around that little bimbo's waist. Was he really that cruel?

"I know we never talked about being exclusive, but I figured if you can sleep in the same bed with *me* all night, the least you could do is stay away from *harlots* during the day." Haley shook with mounting frustration; tears welled up in her eyes.

Trying to calm herself and keep her cool, she took a few deep breaths. He wasn't worth her tears.

When his mouth lifted and a sparkle entered his eyes, she saw red and lifted her hand to smack the grin from his face. He easily caught her and pulled her against his side, finally releasing the woman beside him. And the little winch also happened to be smiling. How punishing could these people be?

Toast. They were toast.

"Haley, I'd like you to meet my sister, Brielle."

It took several heartbeats for Crew's words to sink in, and once they did, Haley's face flamed. Now he would know for sure how crazy she was. She couldn't even look in the chuckling woman's eyes. She'd just called his sister a whore. Who did that?

"It's nice to meet you, Haley. Don't worry about it; I know what a rake my brother can be. You have every right to assume the worst, though I will tell you, he was just gushing about you five seconds before you walked up in all your terrifying glory." Brielle stuck out her hand.

Suddenly unable to speak, Haley met Brielle's outstretched hand and shook it, feeling like a fool. It was Crew's fault — she just couldn't quite figure out how. Never before had she wished for a natural disaster, but she was praying for a hurricane to appear instantly and carry her off deep into the sea. Or a boiler could blow up…

"Sorry," she finally mumbled when her wish wasn't granted and the sky remained clear.

"My father wanted to surprise me by showing up out of the blue. Last time we chatted, he just said he was coming sometime. I figured he'd give me notice, but he likes to pop up unannounced. This is my dad, Richard," he introduced.

"It's a pleasure to meet you, Ms. Sutherland. As Brielle told you, Crew was speaking highly about you moments before you appeared. I hope you will be joining us this evening for dinner so we can get to know you better." The twinkle in his eyes looked familiar, but Haley couldn't trust anything she was seeing right now. She could barely meet the man's eyes, let alone try to figure out why he looked like someone she'd met before.

Haley would rather be dropped off a cliff than spend time with the people she'd just insulted, but she nodded and smiled, trying furiously to think of any excuse to go running back into the resort. She'd bury herself under a mound of blankets and inhale a gallon of ice cream.

"Excellent. Our family has much to talk about and much to celebrate," Richard said, taking her nod for affirmation, and then looking back at his son.

Haley spoke a bit too brightly. "That's wonderful. I really have to be getting back inside. I'll let you all catch up," she said, tugging against Crew, ready to make her escape.

"Mmm, I like this jealous streak. Maybe you can punish me later," he whispered in her ear, making her cheeks heat all over again. "Too bad the anklet doesn't fit *me*."

How could he say that in front of his family? Even if they couldn't hear, she was terrified they knew exactly what he was whispering in her ear.

Without another word, she managed to untangle herself from Crew's arms, and she fled inside.

She wasn't coming out again for another ten years. Maybe her blush would have faded by then. She doubted it, but miracles did come true sometimes.

Chapter Twenty-Two

It wasn't often that Crew didn't have a word to say, but this was too much for him. How could it be possible? Things like this happened only in fiction, not in real life.

"I understand your shock, son," Richard said. "I couldn't believe it myself, but it *is* true. Signed, sealed, delivered, and scientifically verified. I didn't want to give you news like this over the telephone, and I certainly didn't want to tell you until I knew it was fact. We've already spoken to Ashton, Tanner and Lance. Brielle was the stop right before we came here. She insisted on joining us."

Still, Crew sat there and stared at these men, these near duplicates of his father — his uncles. As the oldest child, Crew had always wanted more family when he was younger, cousins to play with, tell secrets to, and run amok with. Now that he was a grown man, he was finding out they'd been there all along, on the other side of the USA.

His family had taken vacations in California, had been through Seattle. He could have sat next to his cousins at a table, and never known. It was all so overwhelming.

"You're taking it about as well as my oldest boy, Lucas, did," Joseph said. The booming sound of his voice finally snapped Crew out of his shock.

"I'm sorry I'm being so disrespectful. I…it's just a lot to take in," he murmured.

"Well, of course it is, boy. It's not every day you find out you have aunts and uncles, and a heck of a lot of cousins. We've planned a family gathering so you can meet. They will love you all as if you've known each other since day one. Family means everything to George and me. Plus, it's been a real privilege for us to meet our brother, Richard. We want to know our new niece and nephews."

The way this larger-than-life man instantly accepted a new family as his own was humbling. How many years had Crew taken family for granted? How many times had he gone off and not once thought of calling his siblings? It had been only after his father's ultimatum that he'd pulled himself together — finally seeing what he had to lose.

Not the money. Sure, at first, that had been the worst of it, but when he and his siblings had sat down to plot against their old man, something else had happened. They'd bonded again — a bond that had been stretched thin over the years, but never broken. Now, they spoke at least once a week. They knew what was happening in each other's lives. They were a family again, leaning on each other for moral support during the difficult undertaking of transforming troubled businesses.

Now, they had even more family, and Crew wanted to meet them all.

"When is the soonest we can do this?"

"I want everyone there for Thanksgiving. It's my favorite holiday because that's when I get to look around an abundant table and count my blessings. I hope you'll plan on it," Joseph replied.

"Yes, of course," Crew responded.

"There's an extra setting for your spitfire girlfriend, too," Joseph said, sending Richard a wink.

Crew looked incredulously from Joseph to his father and then burst out laughing. Despite being apart their entire lives, the men were more alike than seemed possible. Was matchmaking in the family genes? Next Joseph would be yammering on about grandbabies... No. Not likely. No one could be as bad as his dad was when it came to pushiness for the next generation to be born.

"I will consider that," he said, refusing to satisfy the old meddlers' obvious curiosity. Let them sweat. Yes, he was in love with Haley, but she was still frightened. He was waiting for the right moment to tell her she was never escaping him. She could run and she could hide, but he would never let her get away.

"Stubborn. That's definitely Anderson blood," George grumbled.

Crew sat back smugly, pulled out a cigar and lit it.

"Well, don't be selfish there, boy. Offer your uncles one, too," Joseph bellowed. With a laugh Crew handed over cigars to all three men.

"Disgusting habit," Brielle said as she moved her chair away from the smoke.

"You don't know what you're missing out on, Brielle. These are magnificent, came to me all the way from Colombia."

"I'm done with this testosterone-filled room. I think I'll find your girlfriend, Crew, and see what dirt I can get on you. I have a few stories to tell her, too."

Crew considered trying to stop her, but knew he'd be wasting his time or worse. His sister was a force of nature, and when she went after something, it was dangerous to stand in her way.

Instead, he sat back and whipped his head to and fro, listening to the three brothers bantering together as if they'd never spent a day apart. His father wouldn't be lonely ever again.

*****

Brielle took her time exploring her brother's resort. She couldn't deny feeling a bit of jealousy that his project was a luxury hotel, while she was stuck on a ranch.

Then she smiled, for there was nothing at all to pout about. She wouldn't trade places with Crew if she could. She'd never admit that ranch life was suiting her, but her incredibly hot neighbor was certainly a plus in keeping her in the wilds of Montana.

215

She'd let her neighbor come milk her...cows anytime!

As she passed the bar, a curious sound caught her attention. Inching the door open, she slipped inside the dimly lit room, then stood by the back wall as she watched Haley in the corner of the room with her long fingers stroking the keys of the piano.

The poor woman was doing a terrible job of playing, but the man behind the bar didn't seem to mind in the least. When he spotted Brielle, he walked over.

"Sorry, we aren't open for another two hours," he said kindly as he motioned for the door.

"I'm here to see Haley," Brielle said.

The man's eyes narrowed protectively, which had Brielle's curiosity piqued. Who was this woman who had the men in her life so ready to spring to her defense? Brielle was determined to figure it out.

"What business do you have with Ms. Sutherland?"

"I promise you it's nothing bad. Let me introduce myself before you call for the bouncers. My name's Brielle Storm — Crew's baby sister." She stuck out her hand, and after a moment's pause, the man's shoulders relaxed.

"Marlin. It's good to meet you."

"You don't have a last name, Marlin?" Brielle asked with a low chuckle.

"Yeah, but I don't like it. Just call me Marlin. I'll leave you ladies for a few minutes. I have to run to the back anyway to let the guys know what to bring out." With that, the man slipped out the door. Haley hadn't noticed their exchange as she continued to fumble with the chords on the piano.

The girl had also decided to sing, and Brielle didn't know which was worse, the piano playing, or her singing. She wouldn't be winning a Grammy anytime soon, though she certainly was enthusiastic.

Now it was time to get to the bottom of what was going on between her and Crew. From the steam flying between Haley and her brother, Brielle strongly suspected she was more than just a girlfriend. Was this woman worthy of her brother? A feeling deep in her gut told her *yes*.

"I hope I'm not interrupting you," Brielle said as she came out of the shadows. Haley hit the keys with a jolt, thus ending her "song" with an impressive array of discordant notes. Brielle could see Haley had been hoping her hiding spot would hold, but when Brielle wanted something, nothing would stop her, and right now she wanted to find out who Haley was and exactly what she stood for.

"No. Of course not. I'm not really supposed to be in here, but the bar's closed right now. Marlin lets me sneak in because I enjoy playing around on the piano, though I'm obviously terrible at it. I took a class in college on music appreciation and picked up the basics. The instructor, who played beautifully, taught me a few simple songs." Haley neglected to mention the impressive piano in her grandparents' house — after all, she'd been forbidden to touch it while they were alive.

"I know 'Frosty the Snowman,' and 'Silent Night.' My father always insists on Christmas carols around the piano, so each of us were required to learn a couple of songs," Brielle said with a hopeful grin. She sat down on the bench beside Haley and started plunking out "Frosty" since Haley was too shocked to play right then.

"What are the songs Crew knows?" Haley asked, her eyes wide and mouth agape.

"'The Drummer Boy' and 'Friendly Beasts.'"

"I love both of those songs. I'll have to see if he'll play them for me," she said with excitement and delight.

"Well, if you're planning on coming for Christmas, you'll hear him," Brielle said slyly and watched Haley's reaction.

There was hope in the girl's face, true hope that she would still be with Crew at Christmas. The worry in Brielle's chest evaporated when she saw how smitten this woman was.

"That's several months away," Haley said, gathering herself together quickly and looking down at the keys.

"Well, I wanted to seek you out to make sure you'll be there for dinner tonight. I want you to know that I thought you were great not letting Crew get away with anything. If I had been some floozy instead of his sister, you probably would have clawed my eyes out."

Reddening, Haley glanced over at Brielle, then plunked a few keys with Brielle in a terrible rendition of "Silent Night."

"I don't know why I got so upset," she murmured. "It's not like we've ever said this is something official. We've only been together a couple of months now…"

"I think you got so upset because you like my brother — as hard as that is to believe — and maybe even love him."

Haley now blanched, and Brielle knew without a doubt that she'd just met her future sister-in-law. She and Crew were crazy about each other. Now, they just had to admit it, and Brielle would have her first sister-in-law.

"I…uh…don't love him," Haley said. "It's complicated, but he's been helping me with some stuff. Men like Crew marry debutantes or Ivy League girls. They may date women like me, but they marry ladies."

"What do you mean?"

Haley's pain-filled words tore at Brielle's heart.

"I'm not exactly in the same class as Crew — as you. I'm not too stupid to realize that. I enjoy him, and he's been wonderful to me, but this is a summer thing, nothing more. We're just having fun," she trailed off.

Brielle studied her, wanting to know this woman's secrets, wanting to know what had happened in her life that had filled her with so much insecurity.

Guilt consumed her as she thought back to all those years she'd been nothing but a rotten little brat. She'd taken everything she'd been given for granted — the best education, the best clothes, a new car for her sixteenth birthday, everything she'd ever wanted. How shallow she'd been. What a waste of life.

Here was a woman who'd obviously had so much less, yet she was proud and strong and doing it on her own. Brielle had a feeling the two of them would be close friends, and she herself would be the one to gain by the friendship.

"Haley, you should know that love doesn't care about your rank in life. It doesn't care where you went to school, or if you can play the piano. Love is magical and honest and it will find you whether you want it to or not. Don't give up on yourself, because it's pretty obvious to me that my brother thinks you're about the classiest girl out there."

"I…uh…" Haley couldn't speak.

"I adore my brother. He and my other three brothers always spoiled me rotten — quite rotten, I'm afraid, but that's a story for another time. I just wanted to meet the woman he's obviously fallen in love with."

Brielle beamed to see Haley's mouth drop open. If nothing else, she'd gotten the wheels in Haley's head spinning. Sometimes men were big buffoons who just didn't know how to express themselves, and women had to take matters into their own hands. In fact, she knew of one particular man in Montana who could benefit from hearing her thoughts.

"I won't keep you any longer, Haley, but I really do hope to see you tonight at dinner. It's been a real pleasure speaking with you." With that, Brielle got up and left the flustered woman alone. Haley had a lot to think about, and Brielle was hoping for a winter wedding.

There was nothing like snow-covered ground when two people joined their lives together. The new bride and groom were literally forging a new path for themselves from the moment they stepped from the warmth of the church and made their way home — their footprints marking their progress in the pure white snow.

Yes, despite a few bumps in her own road, Brielle was a romantic. It was grand to be herself again and even grander to have her family back, all close-knit and full of love.

Smiling giddily to herself as she made her way toward her room, she didn't even notice the men stopping in their tracks to gaze at her. She knew she was attractive — she wasn't stupid —but she had no idea of the full power she possessed.

Chapter Twenty-Three

OK, she was in love. Hopelessly, irrevocably and forever in love. Haley's heart glowed with warmth as she watched the three men sip on their scotch and fill the room with cigar smoke and raucous laughter. They were a riot and she couldn't get enough of them.

"That's four of a kind. I win!" Haley pulled the pile of Skittles candies toward herself. She'd more or less cleaned them out.

"I think you've been cheating, young lady," Joseph said with a mock pout as he put down his lowly two pair.

"You, my kind sir, are being a poor loser," she taunted.

"If only I wasn't so in love with my Katherine, I'd fight my new nephew for your affections."

"I could fight Katherine for you," Haley said with a wink, loving the soft pink glow in his cheeks.

"Ah, young lady, you do know how to make an old man feel young." He leaned over and kissed her cheek.

The men had been at the resort for a week, and she sought them out regularly when Crew was busy running his resort. The potential buyers were there, and they'd made an official offer. It looked as if her time in paradise was nearly at its end.

She would miss this place beyond expression, but at least she'd have amazing memories to take home with her. The steamy nights with Crew, and this precious week with his father and his new uncles. It was as if she was getting a taste of what a normal family was like and oh how she longed for such.

What a story, a beautiful story — triplets reunited after more than sixty years. And a few days was all it had taken for them to bond. Haley was delighted that both Joseph and George were happily married men, and she simply didn't understand how Crew's father could be single.

Richard was suave and adventurous, and had a devilish attitude. She could certainly see where Crew had inherited not only his good looks, but also his casual but polished manners. She was in over her head with this Anderson/Storm family.

And when she didn't get to see any of them anymore…?

"I've always said a woman who can gamble is a force to be reckoned with. We are leaving in two days, but I expect you to come and visit us, young lady," George said as he looked her in the eye.

Haley didn't want to ruin the mood.

"I think you only want to earn back your candy. You keep trying, but you just can't beat me," she joked as she lifted a few brightly colored pieces and slid them into her mouth.

"You quit trying to change the subject," Joseph pointedly replied, not fooled by her tactics. "You've yet to tell me you'll be there for Thanksgiving. It's only a couple months away and I like a lot of pretty ladies sitting around my table."

"I will come if I can," she said without elaboration. She so wanted to say she'd be there, but she had to remember that this wasn't her family. She was simply borrowing them for a very short time.

"Yes, Haley, I want you to be there, as well. You have brought a sparkle to my ornery son's eyes that I haven't seen in years. You're good for him," Richard said. He was the quietest of the three brothers, but that didn't dim his power in the least.

"That's because I give him so much trouble. Now, if you want to run away with me, we can find a deserted island and hide away forever," she added with a wink, making Richard blush.

"Oh, if I were thirty years younger, I'd throw you over my shoulder and take you to paradise any time," he said with a laugh; Joseph and George joined in.

"This one's taken, Dad," Crew said, surprising Haley with his quiet approach. She peered up at his smiling features.

"Doesn't mean I can't duel you for her," Richard told his son.

"I would be sure to lose to such a smooth man," Crew said before lifting Haley from her chair and seizing her mouth with his so swiftly that she didn't have time even to think about protesting.

As his lips covered hers, she forgot about her three favorite men and melted into her lover's arms. Losing all sense of time or place, she just held on for the ride as he made her body soar.

"Now, that's a kiss," Richard said with a chuckle. Haley plummeted back to solid ground. It was her turn to blush as Crew slowly released her.

"I hate to take Haley away, but I have plans that don't involve three meddlesome men," Crew said as he clasped her hand. Haley tried to pull back, uneasy at the wicked gleam in his eye.

"Thatta boy. You give this girl some good romance. And don't you dare let her go. I didn't raise a fool for a son," Richard said.

Joseph emphatically agreed. "A good woman is not something to treat lightly. You hold on tight and pray she never lets you go. I've been with my Katherine for over forty years now, and not a day goes by that I'm not grateful to have found her."

"Yes, I've been blessed by having two great loves in my life. The last ten years with Esther have been a blessing, and I don't know what I'd do without her," George added.

"I'd give anything to have a woman to hold my heart close to hers. I haven't given up," Richard added with sadness.

"Don't you worry, Brother! We'll find you a bride," Joseph said with excitement.

"Oh, no you won't, Joseph. If love finds me, then it does, but I don't need my brothers meddling in *my* life," Richard said with a glare.

"You three argue about it. I'll see you tonight." With that, Crew picked Haley up in his arms and left the room. The sound of the men whistling followed them to the door.

Crew's he-man act embarrassed her, but she melted against him. The strength of his arms as they flexed beneath her back, the feel of his tight abs pressing against her side, and the look of hunger in his eyes had her breath trapped in her throat.

"You are in quite the mood, aren't you?" she teased as he rounded a corridor behind the bar and headed to his office.

"I've missed you," he answered simply.

Her heart warmed at the thought.

"I like spending time with your dad and uncles. They are stubborn and ornery and I love every minute of it."

"I love being with them, too, but right now I'm going to love being with you," he said as he walked through his office door, quickly shutting it and latching it behind him.

After he put her down on his desk, his mouth quickly seized hers, and she forgot all about scotch, poker, and amusing old threes of a kind. Hunger washed through her as Crew unbuttoned her blouse, exposing her lace bra within seconds.

"Well, why didn't you just say so?" she gasped as his mouth moved down her throat, and then sucked a hardening nipple through the delicate lace. She leaned back and cried out in pleasure.

He was moving quickly, and Haley wouldn't have had it, or him, any other way. She wanted him to take her fast and hard, make her scream in pleasure again and again.

His hand found her front clasp and released her breasts so he could stroke them, tease them, and make her stomach ripple with need.

Running his arm across the surface of the desk, he flung everything there to the floor, then lay her down, unbuttoning her skirt and yanking it and her panties free, leaving her bare before him.

"I can't ever get over how breathtaking you are. I look upon you and wonder how I ever got to be the lucky one who gets to bury myself deep within your heat, kiss every delicate piece of your skin, and then hold you all night while you dream of tomorrow," he whispered, his eyes slowly moving across her body.

Oh, my gosh, the man knew what to say. She was a quivering mess as he ran his hands up her thighs and pushed them apart, leaving her wide open for his hungry gaze.

Suddenly his mouth descended, and she did indeed cry out when he fastened on to her swollen womanhood and turned her heat into an inferno. Lying back on her elbows, she called out his name as he stroked her flames higher, bringing her to the brink of pleasure before…stopping.

"Kiss me," he demanded as he moved up her body, his clothing gone. When on earth had that happened? She didn't know.

Instead of plundering her mouth as he'd done earlier — which she happened to like, a lot —he hovered over her, lightly brushing his lips across hers as his hands framed her face. The sweet moment brought tears to her eyes.

Heat and passion she could take, and take, and take. This loving, slow exploration of her mouth and mind dropped her to her knees. Trying not to shout her love for him, she deepened the kiss, knowing he was close to losing all control.

"I need you, Haley. I always need you," he said as he aligned their bodies together. As he rested the thick head of his erection against her for just a moment, their eyes connected, and they were one.

She was his for the taking, and she wouldn't let go until the moment he forced her to.

Flames ripped through her again as he slowly sank deep within her folds, and then pounded against her flesh, rocking her closer and closer to the edge of pure pleasure. She felt the muscles in his back flexing as he pushed inside her, and she sucked in his moans of desire as their tongues twined together.

The faster and harder he thrust against her, the louder she cried out. More. Always more. She couldn't get enough of him.

Just before she came apart, Crew lifted his mouth and looked deep into her eyes. "Mine, Haley. You are mine. Today. Tomorrow. The day after. I won't let you go."

228

She tried to refuse his words, tried to not let them plant within her heart, but as they shattered together, she felt her tears threatening to spill. Yes. She wanted to be his forever.

But wasn't that what people said in the heat of passion? They felt emotions on a much deeper level, but those emotions burned out swiftly. Still, she allowed herself to cherish a tiny hope of forever as he wrapped her in his arms and carried her to his oversized chair in the corner, holding her as she pulled herself together.

Maybe she wouldn't have to let him go. Maybe her today would last an eternity.

Chapter Twenty-Four

"What are you so afraid of, Haley?"

Grabbing her shirt and covering herself, she turned away as she searched for her panties. Where were the stupid things? There was no way she would leave this office without them and risk the embarrassment of having a resort maid suck them up into her vacuum.

It had been bad enough when they'd been caught making out in the sauna like a couple of teenagers. She'd been utterly mortified. Crew, darn him, had just sat back with a big grin on his face while his poor employee had run from the room with excuses and a flushed face. But really, why was she thinking of that incident now?

Probably because she was afraid to face the conversation he was attempting to have. If she opened up to him only to be let down, she would be hurt, just as she always was. He had a family he could lean on — she had nobody. Why couldn't he understand that?

Even knowing all along it wasn't smart to do anything with him other than take him on as a teacher, she'd still managed to let her heart get involved. So now she was scrambling to build up some sort of defense against the inevitable pain.

He was selling the resort, probably in a matter of days, and after the sale closed, he'd move on to his next big adventure and she'd be by herself again. She used to deal with that just fine, but that was before meeting Crew.

"I'm not afraid of anything, Crew. I like the way things are with us, and I don't see why you keep pushing me," she finally said when he blocked the door.

"What is wrong with admitting that we're good together?" His face was earnest, but she'd shared so much already. What would he think if he knew the depth of her feelings? He was the man out for a good time — not a happily-ever-after.

"We *are* good together. I don't deny that," she said, giving him something so he'd hopefully let the subject drop. She tried to make her tone light, but her soaring stress levels weren't making it easy.

"I love being with you, Haley," he told her as he grabbed her from behind and slid his hand around her waist, his fingers spanning across the flat of her stomach as he pulled her back against his chest. The way his thumb rested just below her breast had her body heating up again.

This was unbelievable torture. She needed some time to think — to pull herself together, and to try to figure out what all of this meant.

"And I love being with you, too, Crew. I do, honestly. I just don't think we should try and put a label on what we have. We're both in an unstable point in our lives and this is supposed to be fun and carefree. You're my teacher, remember?" she said with an attempt at humor.

It fell flat.

"Do you want poems and chocolates?" he asked, sincerely perplexed. "I'm not being sarcastic, Haley. I need to know."

The genuine confusion in his voice almost melted her. He was so good to her, anticipating her needs, caring about how she felt, and making her body sing for him. If only she could hold on to him forever.

"Doesn't every woman?" she laughed as she turned in his arms and slid her lips across his in slow motion.

"Done. I'll clear out the candy shop and have a poet flown in tonight."

She wished she knew whether he was kidding or not.

"How about you just surprise me with a large Dove Bar and we don't stalk writers," she replied while his hands slid down her back. Then he took hold of her head and turned her gentle caress of the lips into a full-scaled attack on her mouth. It looked as if she'd done a good job of distracting him; she didn't know, however, whether to be happy at her success.

When his phone rang just then, Haley felt a mixture of relief and frustration. Her body had just begun to warm up again, but she was glad that she could escape this awkward conversation.

"You take your call, and I'll go for a swim," Haley told him. Fire was just starting to flare in his eyes, so she retreated several feet, to keep temptation from winning her over.

She'd made it to the door before his voice stopped her. "Haley." He paused while she turned. "This conversation is far from over."

As she left the office, she felt fear battle with hope. The hope was more terrifying. If she let herself think of a real future with him, she'd be swimming without a life jacket in the middle of a stormy ocean, and it would probably be easier to just give in and let the water drag her under.

With a shake of her head, she suppressed her confused tears and made her way to their suite to change. A good swim and workout would put her mind back on track. That was all she needed, she convinced herself.

*****

Crew got off the phone, and then rested his head in his hands. He knew and understood her fears of the future, but he'd hoped she'd have a bit more trust in him by now. He would give her a week or two to work through her emotions, and then he'd pounce.

Haley had changed his life for the better; he couldn't possibly let her go now. Did everyone have a one perfect mate out there somewhere? He only knew that without her, his life would be emptier.

The two of them could have a good life together. Her insecurity still held her back, but over the last couple of months, he'd watched as she'd come alive, opened up and faced so many of the demons that littered her past.

One by one, she was slaying her dragons, and he vowed to be there fighting by her side.

Chapter Twenty-Five

Crew ended up giving Haley a break for only a day. He'd planned to give her more time, but he had news, and he couldn't wait to tell her.

His lawyers and those hired by the buyers had pushed through the paperwork, and he needed to let Haley know that at the end of the month it was time to move on. He hoped she wouldn't mind going off with him to a new location. Though she had her schooling to finish, she was taking this semester off, and he'd find her the best school possible. What was important to her was important to him, too.

Crew had decided that his next business venture was going to be in Oregon. There was a great resort on the beaches of Tillamook, and he wanted to restore it. He'd be closer to his newfound family and get to know the cousins he'd never met.

Haley should love it there. The weather was almost identical to that in Seattle, plus she'd still be on the beach, he reasoned.

This kind of news required a candlelit dinner with at least a few dozen roses, and a lot of chocolate. Women, he'd theorized, were a lot more likely to listen if they had good chocolate in their hands. Haley had certainly proved that often.

A flashback to one night when they'd experimented with chocolate syrup and whipped cream flooded his memory, and Crew lost his train of thought. *Dammit.* Shaking his head, he got back to work. There was a lot to plan, and it needed to be just right.

"Mr. Storm."

"Mr. Storm."

Crew turned to find the Stanther twins wobbling toward him. The two old ladies were in their eighties and full of life, though doubtless a bit slower than they'd been in years gone by.

They must have been true beauties in their day. Knowledge and laughter glowed in their eyes, and he'd delighted in having them at the resort for the past week. He rarely became attached to guests, but he'd made an exception with the two spitfires.

"How can I help you beautiful ladies?" he said as he gave each woman a kiss on the hand.

"Oh, you're such a charmer. If I had the energy that I used to," Bertha Stanther said, "I'd drag you up to my nice big suite with me. It's just too bad age has caught up to me."

"Ah, age has made you only more striking," he said with a wink.

The two ladies giggled, and soft blushes stole over their cheeks. Penelope now spoke: "We just wanted to say goodbye. Our grandnephew is picking us up today and taking us back home. We've so enjoyed our time with you, Mr. Storm. I do hope to see you again in a couple of months."

"Sadly, I won't be here, ladies. But when I get my next resort up and running, you have a free week on me," he promised, handing them each his personal business card.

"Ooh, we'll certainly take you up on that. A free vacation sounds divine," Bertha said. The women were dripping in jewels and had more money than they'd ever need to spend, but they'd been through hard times in their lives, and pinched pennies where it counted. He was honored to give them a week vacation at his cost.

"You'd better come, because I will miss you both. How about a kiss?" He leaned down so each of them could give him a pink-lipstick-stained kiss on his cheek.

"We'll see you soon, Mr. Storm," they called out as they turned to walk toward the nicely dressed young man who gave each of them a hug and began asking how their trip had been. Crew hoped to see them again. He really had enjoyed their sense of humor and positive attitudes. Neither of them was letting age stop them from enjoying life, and he hoped he was just the same when he hit his eighties.

After watching the sisters safely escorted away, Crew turned to hunt down his father and uncles. His family was leaving the next day and, though he hated to confess it, the ease with which they'd snuck into Haley's heart made him the slightest bit jealous.

Every moment she could find, she was with the three old men, and she and his sister had really hit it off, even teaming up with some of his staff to cause chaos for him.

He couldn't be angry, though, because Haley had no family, no friends — no one. That was before he'd entered her life, of course; now she'd never be alone again.

Each day he was with her, he fell further in love. The deepest desire of his heart was to hold on tight and never let her go. And, yes, he would miss the meddling old men once they departed, but he had a feeling Haley would miss them even more.

Crew was hardly surprised to find the three of them sitting at the bar, visiting with his favorite bartender, with whom they'd hit it off quickly. Not a shocker, since both they and Marlin swore by fine booze and expensive cigars. Crew had decided already to offer Marlin a job package too good to refuse if he came to the next resort with him.

"Last I checked, this was a place of business," Crew said, trying to sound gruff, but not pulling it off.

"Oh, quit your bellowing and join us for a smoke," his father said as he scooted his chair over a bit so Crew could sit down. At this time in the afternoon, there were few patrons, and Crew had a chance to relax.

"Don't mind if I do," he said accepting a cigar from his Uncle Joseph and lighting up. Leaning back in the chair, he noticed that all eyes were on him. The men were looking at him as if they'd weighed him and found him wanting.

"What?" he finally asked, not normally self-conscious, but struggling not to squirm under the heat of their stern gazes.

"We were just discussing you, boy, and wondering what the heck is wrong with you that you haven't asked Haley to be your bride."

Leave it to his father to come right to the point.

"I don't see how that's any of your business. That goes for all of you." Crew pointedly looked each of them in the eye, giving Marlin an extra look for good measure. But the man didn't back down an inch — was Crew losing his touch?

"Well, of course it's our business. We're family and want to make sure you're OK," Joseph bellowed, blowing a thick plume of smoke from his mouth.

Crew had known of the man's existence for only a couple of weeks and yet Joseph was already comfortable in his role as uncle. To Crew's great surprise, he found he didn't mind at all. He felt as if he'd known Joseph and George his entire life, and he was grateful to be a part of their family now.

"Not that I should admit this to any of you, but I won't be letting Haley slip through my fingers. I may have made some stupid decisions in my younger years, but when you get your hands on a woman that good, you certainly don't let her get away."

"And besides, it's about time I had grandkids…" Richard trailed off as Crew's words registered in his ears. A huge smile broke out on his face as he looked at his eldest son.

Crew had never been a pathological people pleaser, but he felt a swell of pride at the slight sheen of tears in his dad's eyes.

"Uh…well…that's very good, Crew. I'm mighty proud of you," Richard finally said as he clapped his boy on the back.

"What are you proud about, Dad?" Brielle asked as she joined them, plopping down in a chair and grabbing Crew's cigar, much to his dismay.

"I thought you hated these," he snapped as he tried to grab it back.

"I'm trying to broaden my horizons," she said and she took in a puff, then doubled over as the smoke clogged her lungs.

"You're not supposed to inhale, darling niece; just taste the sweet smoke on your tongue." George patted her back and offered her some water.

"Thanks for the warning," she gagged with a glare at Crew.

"You didn't give me a chance," he responded with a smirk as he took his cigar back. That would show her to take one of his.

"OK. OK. You got me. So what are you so proud about?" she asked again.

"Crew's getting married," Joseph piped in.

Crew looked around in a panic. "Shh. I haven't talked to Haley about any of this, and no one said anything about marriage. I just said I wasn't going to let her go," he whispered.

"You'd better not plan on just shacking up with the girl. She's a lady and deserves a ring on her finger," George admonished him.

"You guys are so nosy," Crew growled as he stood and smashed out his cigar in the ashtray. He'd best find Haley before the old men gave away his game plan. He would bet his fortune none of them could keep a secret. Why he'd said anything, he didn't know.

"Well, we wouldn't have to be if you weren't such a blasted fool," Richard called out.

Crew didn't bother responding as their laughter followed him from the room. It was a good thing Marlin had kept quiet; otherwise, he might have canned him on the spot.

He wouldn't have, of course, but it was a nice thought, anyway.

With a determined stride, Crew headed to his room. It was time to give Haley the romance she wanted. He had big plans for them, and the tighter he weaved his net, the more likely he'd be able to keep her stuck in it forever.

Chapter Twenty-Six

Several hours later Crew found Haley reading a book out back by one of the fire pits. He loved the way her face lit up when she came to a good part in a story, and the different ways her tears would fall during joyous and sorrowful scenes.

He didn't even need to pick up the book. He could read it through her expressions alone. If only she were as easy to read when they talked. She had grown very good at masking her emotions in front of him.

He hoped by the end of the night she'd trust him enough never to do that again.

"Good evening, beautiful," he said as he sat next to her and nuzzled her neck.

"Hi, Crew. Sorry I haven't come up yet. I lost track of time."

"It wasn't too hard to find you. Are you ready?"

"Yes. I'm getting sleepy."

Helping her stand, he wrapped his arm around her and began leading her toward the elevators.

"Did you have a good day?"

"Yes. I went golfing for the first time in my life. It's a good thing your father and uncles are so patient; I was afraid they might throw me into one of the water traps. I'm terrible at it," she told him with a laugh. "Correction. I'm very good at finding the water traps."

"I'll tell you a little secret. I'm terrible, too."

He could see she didn't believe him.

"You know those old men are crazy about you. I thought there for a while that I might have to fight my father for you. He's pretty infatuated."

"Oh, I love them, Crew. They are all so funny and kind. Whenever I dreamed of having a father, I imagined him being the perfect mixture of all three of them. They may bark pretty loudly, but they all have hearts of gold, and are really just big softies," she said with a sigh.

Crew was grateful she loved his family so much. Now that he'd found his way back home again, he could never settle down with a woman who didn't think family was just as important as their relationship. They went hand in hand.

If you had family, Crew believed, but no one by your side to love, you were only half a person. It went both ways, though. If you had true love, but no family to come home, too, you were still only half a person. To feel the full effect of a happily-ever-after, you needed your true love and your family to keep you

243

standing strong. They were the ones who'd hold your hand in a storm, fall to their knees with you when the rest of the world let you down — they were everything that made you a whole person.

Poor Haley had gone so many years without that special bond. And though he'd had it all along, for years he'd taken for granted those who mattered most. At least it wasn't too late for either of them.

They reached the room, and he slowly opened the door and ushered her inside. She stopped in her tracks.

Crew was proud of himself. Since he wanted to uproot her life, he'd gone all out to make this night special, do it the correct way. Nothing but scented candles lit the room; they cast dancing shadows on the wall and released the sweet scent of jasmine in the air.

A table was set in the middle of the room with silver and crystal and the finest bottle of champagne he could get his hands on. A menu of cold salad, lobster fettuccine and chocolate mousse was ready to be served when they were, and overflowing vases of flowers sat on the two end tables. A few roses lay across her plate.

"What is the occasion?" she asked in a whisper. She looked up at him with gleaming eyes.

Yes, he'd done well, he thought as he pulled her close.

"Every day I'm with you is an occasion to celebrate," he told her, surprised by how much he meant the words.

"Crew, you make me melt," she said as she kissed him in appreciation.

Before he got lost in her touch, he led her to the table, where he picked up one of the delicate flutes and poured a glass of the sparkling wine.

"To yesterday, today, and tomorrow. May each and every day we face be as magical as this very moment," he offered as a toast, and she clinked her glass against his.

He held out her chair and had her sit, then moved around to the other side of the table so he could relish her every expression and gesture. When he watched her pick up her fork with her long, slender fingers and begin to nibble on her salad with her luscious mouth and tiny white teeth, moaning her approval, his body had no choice but to tighten.

He had to remind himself again that there was a purpose to this night. Yes, he planned on getting her into bed afterward, but he needed her to accept his offer to move with him. He refused to leave the island without her.

Feeling the inside of his pocket, where a small velvet box rested against his heart, he couldn't believe he was working up a sweat. Why on earth was he so nervous?

Because, for once in his life he was going into something to which he didn't know the outcome. He normally never gambled on anything; he was all about guaranteed wins. With Haley, although he felt that she loved him, what if he were simply seeing what he so desperately wanted to see?

She spoke of her fears, but Crew found himself the one now afraid — afraid of losing her. It was unthinkable.

"The resort has sold," he told her. "The papers were signed today and the new owners will take over at the end of this month."

Haley's fork clattered to her plate. She quickly picked it back up and threw him one of her trademark fake smiles.

"That is wonderful, Crew. I'm very happy for you," she said, her voice almost convincing.

He didn't understand why she was upset. He'd told her for months this was in progress. Was she *that* attached to Catalina Island? If she was, he could most likely find another development property nearby. Not on the island, as he'd signed a non-compete clause, saying he wouldn't build another resort there that could possibly be better than this one. But the California mainland was only twenty-two miles away, and he could easily commute to another spot on the coastline to do what was now his passion, restoration.

"Is everything OK, Haley? You seem a little...I don't know..."

"I'm very happy for you, Crew. Very happy," she said, rising from the table. When her arms twisted around his neck and she sat on his lap, he didn't fight her; nor did he when her lips moved over his.

But after a few moments, he pulled back and tried to get the situation under control. Sex would come later. Right now, he had a very important question.

"Make love to me," she pleaded, and she wiggled herself against him. This was hard; he was hard.

Harder. Hardest. No! He couldn't do this right now. He had to think. The night was planned out for a reason.

"Haley…" he groaned as her breasts pushed into his chest and her fingers began undoing his shirt.

"No more talking, Crew. Make love to me," she demanded as she slipped from his lap and knelt before him, unbuttoning his pants and freeing his pulsing arousal.

He intended to stop her, even moved his hands to her hair to push her away, but as her sweet, hot mouth circled over him, his head fell back in ecstasy.

Afterward. They'd talk afterward…

Chapter Twenty-Seven

Crew woke up alone in the bed. The sheets were cold where Haley normally slept, and a sense of unease filled him.

He'd lost his head for a while last night, totally and completely lost it. Yet how could he refuse her when she was begging him to make love to her? He'd never claimed to be a saint and she'd pushed him beyond the limits of what he could possibly handle.

He'd gladly do it all over again. She'd been spectacular.

Wait. Now Crew was sitting up quickly in bed. No matter how good it had been, it wasn't even close to worth it if she'd somehow managed to sneak out on him. He'd felt her pulling away, and should have been thinking of more than his sexual needs. He needed Haley in his life.

Relief whooshed through him when he discovered all her things still there in the room. She hadn't left him, not yet, at least.

He knew she was planning to run, but he wasn't going to let her get far. She'd put him under her spell last night, but even if he had to find a damned chastity belt for himself, he wasn't going to let her pull that trick again until the ring in his pocket was on her beautiful finger. Hello, cold showers.

*****

Haley's Cinderella-size feet enjoyed their shoeless freedom, relishing the feel of the cool wet sand between their toes. She left a pattern behind her as she walked lazily along the beach. She'd gone several miles and it was past time to turn around, but she couldn't bring herself to do it just yet. Last night had been special, something that she could remember Crew by.

She loved him. How could she not when he'd been nothing but kind to her, done nothing but show her how to be a better person? Everything he'd done so far had been about her, for her, and now she owed him his freedom.

She'd be OK. She didn't know how, but she would make it through this. He'd taught her how to respect herself, to be comfortable with the person she was inside. He'd taught her that she was a beautiful woman. Though it wouldn't come easily for her, she would never put on a dunce cap and stand in a corner again. That was all thanks to Crew Storm.

In the far recesses of her mind, she knew she was running away. She knew she was far more afraid of his rejection — of actually hearing him say the words that he didn't want her anymore. If she were the one to walk away, maybe, just maybe, it wouldn't hurt as badly.

After all they'd been through together, if he turned on her, pushed her away from him, she would have a hard time getting past it. She'd been rejected her entire life by those who should have been the first to embrace her. She deserved to be a little weak just this once, didn't she? If she found love ever again — doubtful — and met again with failure — more likely — she would try to face up to rejection head on.

After another half mile, Haley turned around. The sun was rising in the sky, and the last of the morning fog was dissipating, bringing a beautiful new day to the rest of the people on the island. Haley wished the fog around her heart would clear as well, leaving her ready to begin a new life.

She picked up her pace for her return toward the Catalina Couture Resort. It was best to just get this over with. She'd rip off the bandage and then she and Crew could both move forward.

What she wanted next she just didn't know, whether it was to get back into school, move, or keep things the way they'd been before coming to this small paradise. But after their conversation, she simply couldn't stay here any longer. To see him would be heartbreak. Maybe she'd go to Italy and be a tourist, find a job in a small café and try her hand at art.

As she reached the resort and stepped inside the lobby's beautiful French doors, her heart thudded. No matter how she'd tried to prepare herself for what was to come, her heart still ached, and fear climbed higher in her throat.

Somehow she put one foot in front of the other and managed to return the kind smiles of the front-desk associates, and then she walked down the short hallway to his office. Maybe he wouldn't be there and she could just leave him a note, take the coward's way out.

No. She wouldn't do that. After all he'd done for her, he deserved to hear her say goodbye to his face.

Crew was sitting at his desk, his phone held to his ear, when he looked up and saw her in the doorway. A wide grin spreading across his face, he motioned for her to enter.

Why did he have to be so perfect? Why was it that every muscle in her body was urging her to rush into his arms? If he'd been cruel even once, this wouldn't be so difficult.

But then, if he'd been cruel, her heart wouldn't be breaking right now. Trying her best to look upbeat, she moved forward and sat down, crossing her legs and leaning back as she waited for his call to end.

"Sorry about that, Haley. I was planning on looking for you this morning, but then I got called down for an early staff meeting. Since then, I haven't been able to get off the phone for more than five minutes at a time. Where did you go?"

"Oh, I needed to take a walk. It was no big deal. Now I just need to speak to you, for only a minute," she said, adopting a cheerful yet businesslike tone.

"Let me switch the phones over and I'll take you for a late breakfast," he said as he stood up.

"We don't need to do that, Crew. This won't take long. I just wanted to let you know I'm leaving tomorrow. I have everything arranged already and didn't want to take up too much of your time today. I know you have a lot going on with the sale. I need to spend the rest of the day packing, and then I'll be out of your hair before you know it," she said. She refused to acknowledge the tears burning at the bottom of her throat, let alone give in to them.

Crew went from smiling to stone-faced in the span of two seconds. She couldn't read anything in his eyes as he refused to let her look down — refused to break their gaze.

"Would you care to explain further?"

"What do you mean?" she asked, deciding it easiest to play dumb.

"Why the sudden urgency to leave?"

A shiver ran down her spine at the cold fury in his voice. He was pissed and not trying to hide it. Maybe she should have just slipped away during the night.

Not knowing her next move, Haley just sat there, frozen.

*****

Crew was furious. He couldn't remember ever being this angry. He didn't know whether he wanted to haul her into his arms and rip her clothes off, reminding her how good they were together, or to bend her over his knee and smack her on the ass.

As her large green eyes grew wide and he saw the glimmer of insecurity and self-doubt, his temper instantly cooled. She was trying her damnedest to act cool and collected, but she obviously wasn't in as much control as she wanted him to believe.

Something else was going on here, and he was going to find out what.

"Why the sudden desire to run away, Haley? I thought you were finished hiding."

His comment made the color rise in her cheeks; she gazed at him and seemed at a loss for words. Emotions, he could deal with; dead-silence, he couldn't. As long as she wasn't just through with him, he could fix this. And there was just no way he could have been so wrong about her.

Drawing up closer, he took pleasure in the tenseness of her shoulders. She was far from cool, and, with the last of his apprehension fading away, he reached down and lifted her to her feet.

She took a faltering step backward as she tried to regroup, but he didn't give her the opportunity. Tracking her as she bumped up against his desk, he boxed her in, then stood over her.

"I need some space!" she cried as she tried to skirt around him.

"I think I've given you enough room to breathe. I asked a question and I want to know what this is about," he said, his hand rising to trace the contour of her cheek.

She flinched as if his touch were painful.

Good. She was hurting. She didn't want to leave him. His senses were heightened and he picked up on the slightest twitch of her muscles — in her face, her body — as he searched for clues to why she would say something so random and ludicrous.

"This is nothing more than your dignity getting squashed," she huffed. "Fine. If you want to be the one to call it quits, be my guest. We both know you are leaving in a couple of weeks. So, you don't want to lose your easy lay for your remaining time here. Well, too damned bad. I'm going." She ended with just the slightest hitch to her voice.

That was it. She was afraid he would walk away from her. Man, did she have it all wrong. Crew pushed up against her, unashamedly crowding into the last remaining space between them.

"Is that what you think? Do you honestly believe this has all meant nothing to me — that I'm going to just walk away from you without ever looking back?"

"That's what you do, isn't it? You like the ladies, like to wine and dine them, show them a good time, and then walk away. I've heard all the stories. Well, I'm giving you your freedom, Crew. You're free to move on to your next woman," she forced out through gritted teeth.

He rocked his hips forward, brushing his rapidly rising arousal against her, enjoying the shock in her eyes as their bodies connected.

The two of them had never had a problem when it came to sex. She was responding to him as she always did, and he was forced to back off just a hair before he got too turned on and forgot what was most important. That had happened before...

Haley pulled against him, desperately trying to escape his grasp. Crew wasn't having it. He gripped her arm and held on tight. He wasn't letting her go anywhere, not unless she truly wanted to leave him. He was done with her trying to hide from him. He wanted all or nothing from here on out.

"Let me go, Crew. I have things to do."

"What if I don't want to let you go? What if I like you right where you are?" he said with a knowing smirk.

"This is ridiculous. Stop now!" she cried out, on the verge of tears.

Good. They were finally getting somewhere real. "Stop what, Haley? Stop caring about you? Stop making love to you? Stop dreaming of a future with you? Stop loving you? Which emotion, which temptation, which feeling should I stop?"

Her eyes widened as tears filled them, then began trickling down her face.

"Why are you trying to hurt me?" she begged, raw pain flashing across her features.

"I'm not the one wielding the knife, Haley. You are. All I've wanted for the past month was to show you that you can't live without me. I love you. I need you by my side." He didn't see how he could get much clearer than that.

"But, for how long, Crew? You think you love me, but you don't know the real me. You don't know how messed up I really am. I've been on good behavior with you…but I have so many issues, so many problems…"

"I don't care. I love you, Haley."

When she was silent and an innocent hope began filling her eyes, he pressed on. "I love you, Haley." She still said nothing. "Do you understand what I am saying? I love you."

"I…I…how?" she gasped.

"How can I not? You make me want to be a better person. You're kind to strangers, loving and giving. You make me laugh and burn even at the same time. I love you because you make me the person I've always wanted to be, but didn't know how to become. You are special and talented, and it would be my pleasure if you'd stand by my side even when I'm a fool, even when I don't always make the wisest of choices. I want to build a life with you, take you to any and all of the surviving Wonders of the World, make love to you in the ancient pyramids. You make me want to fly and to take you with me."

Crew let her go so he could drop to his knees. Drawing from his pocket the ring he'd been holding onto, he opened the box and held it out to her, his heart hers for the taking.

Haley's body froze as she looked at the box, and gasped. When she finally raised her head to return his gaze, her eyes were overflowing with emotion. Crew had gotten through to her.

The weight on his chest lifted as he looked upon her raw beauty. He'd have the rest of his life to worship her, show her how special she truly was.

"Marry me, Haley. Please say that you will be my wife. Please don't run from me. I can't ever say it enough, but you are my world now."

Haley dropped to her knees to be at eye level with him, and too overcome with emotion to speak, she simply nodded her head, sobbing as he clasped her hand in his and slipped an exquisite diamond in place.

"Is this what you really want?" she finally asked.

"This is the Final Lesson, Haley. Just be yourself, always, and your man will fall to his knees to honor and cherish you."

"I do love you, Crew. I thought I was doing the right thing in walking away, letting you live your life because you've given me more than any other person ever has. But it was ripping me apart to think of never seeing you again." She wound her arms around his neck and laid her head on his shoulder.

It was over — the pain, sorrow and fear was over. Relief and unadulterated love consumed him as he realized he'd never have to be apart from her.

Crew lifted his hand and stroked her hair, holding her as she cried quietly against him. "You will never be alone again, Haley Sutherland. Not only do you have me to love you forever, but you now have the family you always should have had. We will always be there for you."

Raising her head, she gave him a watery smile and thanked him with a gentle kiss before he stood and lifted her into his arms. They would forge that path in the pure snow together, and he'd keep his promises of cherishing her always.

Melody Anne

Chapter Twenty-Eight

"That is absolutely the best engagement sex I've ever had," Crew said with a satisfied grin.

"What?" Haley gasped. The thought that he'd been engaged before pierced her heart.

"I'm just kidding, Haley…well, not about the sex. That was incredible. I'm kidding about engagement sex. You are the one and only woman I've ever wanted to spend the rest of my life with," he appeased her.

Haley relaxed against his chest, grateful he hadn't let her walk away. What a fool she'd been to succumb to her fears. She gazed adoringly at the ring on her left hand, and she couldn't help but think of how far she'd come in the last several months.

At the beginning of the year she'd been taking a psychology course, and thank goodness her professor had suggested the assignment to do something outside their comfort zone. If she'd never gone to that auction, she wouldn't have met the nice man who'd given her a ticket for two weeks at the Catalina Couture…

"Oh, my gosh, I knew I'd seen your father before!" Haley exclaimed as she sat straight up.

"What are you talking about?" Crew looked at her as if she were going mad.

"Your dad. I met him right before coming down here. I was at a charity function…"

"Wait. Slow down. You need to start from the beginning," Crew said, his brows drawn together. So Haley leaned back and began telling him the story…

Nine months earlier

"For your final project, each of you will step out of your comfort zone, and approach a stranger, strike up a conversation, and ask that person three questions. Here are the places you may choose from. You must pick the three questions, but they may not be simple and impersonal, like 'What is your favorite color?'; they have to be complex or personal, such as 'Where did you spend your honeymoon?'"

Haley sat frozen in the chair. How was she supposed to ask a complete stranger intimate questions?

As if the professor could read her mind, he spoke again. "Don't let this overwhelm you. Each of you signed up for my class because something was missing in your lives. You wanted to delve a bit deeper. After this term, each of you will move on to new and exciting adventures. This person you approach will be a stranger whom you will most likely never see again. This is a good test for future job interviews, for your confidence, and for your overall education. If you have any questions, see me after class."

"What exactly are we looking for as a response?" someone asked.

"That is a good question. You are going to take note of their reaction. What is the expression in their eyes? Do they look away as you ask them? Are they open or closed off? Does their jaw tense as if they are uncomfortable, or do they laugh and relax? How you read people is important to how you will later conduct interviews and act in places of business."

"What do you expect on the paper?"

"I want a diagnosis of the emotional state of the stranger. Think of yourselves as psychologists, and the people you question as your patients. Write a five- to seven-page paper on how they respond, not just their answers, but their demeanor. Look beyond the box."

The handout came down Haley's row and she glanced at the short list of events placed before her. She hadn't come so far only to fail, so it looked as if she was going to be putting her newly learned skills to the test.

She chose a charity auction, and felt the first stirrings of unease settle in her stomach. No. She pushed the anxiety away. She could do this.

Leaving the class, she drove to a local mall and wandered around for a while, looking for the most nondescript black dress she could find. It was a strange feeling not to worry about money, but still she was frugal. Years of not knowing what the next day would bring had taught her to be careful. She couldn't change that in the course of a few years. She didn't want to change it.

Never would she be as selfish and bitter as her grandparents.

Finding a dress she could live with, she paid the cashier, then drove home. The event was that night and she figured she'd better get it over with, or else lose her nerve. If that happened, she'd have to try another event, and on and on until no events were left. She could do this.

Taking a little time to apply a spot of blush and some mascara, she threw her hair into a bun and slipped into the dress and low heels, then grabbed a purse and headed back out the door of her apartment.

Arriving at the fundraiser, she found herself in a line of cars waiting for valet parking. It didn't take long for her to reach the front of the line, and she offered a genuine yet nervous smile to the young boy who opened her car door.

"Good evening, ma'am. Have a pleasant night," he said as she handed him a tip and stepped from the car.

Walking through the open double doors on trembling legs, she found herself in a glamorous ballroom, and the butterflies in her stomach nearly flew out of her mouth. To be more exact, she felt as if something were going to come out of her mouth...and it probably wasn't butterflies. There was so much to take in around her.

Men were dressed in impeccably tailored tuxedoes — no rentals here — and women displayed gowns in all styles and colors, though none came close to her sixty-dollar off-the-rack *pièce de résistance*. The amount of sparkle from the diamonds dripping from the women was enough to blind her, but she kept her head high as she scanned the items up for bid.

Though she had enough money to pay for any of the items for sale, she would never spend ten thousand dollars on a one-of-a-kind diamond bracelet or twenty thousand for a night on the town with a Hollywood megastar. She had *so* picked the wrong place to come for her psychology paper.

Just as she was thinking it was time for her to abandon this mission, her eye caught on a poster showcasing an exclusive island resort with blue skies and shining beaches. Intrigued, she moved toward it and found an older gentleman standing nearby.

His expression was friendly; she wondered whether he might be willing to answer a few questions, but her shyness took over and she turned to stare at the advertisement.

It wasn't an auction item, but a vacation won by raffle only. At the end of the night, a name would be drawn, and the winner would spend two weeks at the new resort in Catalina Island when it opened in May. She was tempted to invest a few dollars on the off chance of winning.

"It looks like paradise, doesn't it?"

Haley was startled when the older gentleman spoke. She tentatively glanced up and realized he was speaking to her.

"Yes, it does. After my finals are done, I could use a vacation," she shyly responded.

"Finals? What are you studying?"

This was the perfect opportunity to ask him some questions.

Taking a deep breath, she thought, *Here goes*. "Among other things, I'm taking a psychology class right now."

"I love psychology courses. I remember learning more about *myself* than anything else while there," he replied, and she relaxed.

A soft beard covered his cheeks and chin, and he wore tinted glasses. She wondered why, and thought that would be a good question, but more than a bit rude.

"Yes, I think I've grown over the past four months, though our professor likes to give us assignments that many would consider outside of the box," she said with a slight laugh.

"Ah, I had a few professors like that. What is this man or woman doing to torment you at the moment?"

His easy laughter made Haley feel a bit more comfortable. "I'm supposed to ask questions of strangers," she said nervously.

"Mmm, that sounds interesting."

She couldn't tell whether he would be willing or not, but she had nothing to lose by asking. "Would you mind answering a few for me? Though asking the questions is the entire reason that I'm here tonight, I'd

263

rather die, honestly, than approach people." Her heart pounded as she waited for his response.

"It's never a hardship to speak to a woman as beautiful as you," he suavely replied.

Blushing furiously, Haley pulled out her notepad and a pen. If he thought it strange, he didn't say anything.

She really should have planned better because she didn't have anything written down. She honestly hadn't thought she'd get this far. She'd start off easy, and just ask a few more than the three she was supposed to, then pick and choose what she wrote about in her paper.

"Did you grow up in Seattle?"

"No, I didn't. I was born here, but then my parents moved to the East Coast when I was a young boy. I just recently moved back," he said before asking his own question. "Now it's my turn. Why did it take a college class to get you out here, and why are you all alone?"

Haley was nervous to the point of nausea, but she stifled it and smiled at him. "I don't like public events at all, especially parties like this, though I shouldn't tell you that. I just feel like I'm in far over my head. I'd rather be home in my jammies studying," she answered with a nervous giggle.

"Now you have me intrigued. Tell me more."

"There's not a whole lot to tell. I go to school, work part time, and harass strangers on the side," she tried to joke.

When his lips twitched and a chuckle escaped his mouth, she felt her nausea rise. She couldn't have a sophisticated conversation with a man in a tux. He was so far above her station in life, it wasn't even funny. It didn't matter how much she had in her bank account. That wasn't truly her money; it was an inheritance — and to make it worse, her grandparents were surely rolling over in their graves at the way she was using it. They'd never thought her worthy of going to college, of being anything other than a burden on society.

"Well, we don't want you failing your course, now, do we? Ask me anything else you'd like," he said.

Haley beamed up at him and lifted her notepad back up. "Do you have children?"

A happy smile spread across his features. "Yes. I have five of them, though there are times I want to toss each and every one into the ocean and make them swim back to shore like the Navy Seals do."

"I'm sorry. Are there family problems at home?" Realizing that was far too personal to ask, Haley backed off. When she felt someone was in pain, she wanted to help, since she'd gone through so much of her own trauma, but this man was obviously successful and didn't need her help. "I apologize. That was rude. Please ignore me and let me ask something else."

Before she could say anything further, he cut in. "Yes, there are some problems. My children can be very spoiled. They are doing much better now, but some of us are still struggling a bit. I have faith that it will all work out, however."

"I would have loved having siblings. I *really* would have loved having a mom and dad. Sometimes we aren't given what we truly want, or think we need most, but I think in the end it all works out for the best," she said while lifting her hand and placing it on his arm in a comforting touch. For just a moment, she forgot this man wouldn't want or need her advice, or her comfort.

"What is your name, young lady?"

"Haley Sutherland." She realized she was gripping his arm and instantly tried to remove her hand.

"What other questions do you have for me," he asked while placing his hand over hers. She relaxed, feeling an odd connection with this gentle man.

"What is the one thing you want more than anything else?"

For a brief moment, he was silent, and Haley hoped she hadn't overstepped again.

"I want my children to be happy and married, to have children of their own and to live their lives to the fullest without throwing away their futures," he said with a wistful note in his voice.

"I don't think that's asking for too much. From only speaking to you for a few moments, I have a feeling that you will make a wonderful grandfather." She gave him her best smile, then decided she'd monopolized enough of the kind man's time.

"You are a sweet girl, Haley. Let me give you a small token as an early graduation gift," he said.

"Oh, I have three semesters left," she corrected him, not wanting to accept anything from a stranger who had shown her nothing but kindness.

"Well, that's why it's an early gift. I have a few extra tickets for the drawing for two weeks at the Catalina Couture Resort," he said, placing the tickets in her hand and folding her fingers over them.

To say *no* again would be rude, so Haley smiled up at him, never dreaming that she might win.

"Thank you. You've been very kind." With a smile, Haley turned and wandered around the room. At the end of the night, when her name was called, she was so stunned she didn't know what to think or do.

It wasn't until she was writing up her report that she realized she'd forgotten to get the man's name. It was too late now. She hoped her professor would still accept the paper and not make her suffer through something like that again.

Present time

"That was my dad?"

"Yes, I didn't recognize him when he was here because he was clean shaven and not wearing the glasses, but his voice sounded so familiar that I knew I must have met him before. I just didn't know where."

"Do you think...? No. There's no way..." he trailed off.

"What?" she asked, needing to know why he suddenly looked so full of suspicion.

"He couldn't have fixed that drawing, could he?"

Haley thought about it for a moment and didn't see how that was possible. "No. Why would he want to, anyway?"

"Maybe he was trying to set us up."

"But…he didn't know anything about me. That makes no sense, none whatsoever. Besides, how was he to know my next class was human sexuality and I'd have to approach another stranger and ask for a date?"

"You weren't asking me for the date. You were asking me to teach you how to be with another man," he growled as he pinned her down on the mattress.

"That was the best decision I ever made," she said. How she loved the man who'd taught her so much.

"Yes, it was. Now, I have a few more lessons to teach you…"

He spent the rest of the day teaching her how very much he honored her with his body. *We may as well start the honeymoon now*, she thought with a satisfied smile. Yes, Haley had changed. The shy, frightened girl she'd been was slowly being replaced by this confident woman she was becoming. It was all thanks to the faith of a lonely old man, who happened to like meddling in his children's lives, and of course, thanks to Crew, who would forever be her true love for always having confidence and faith in her.

Epilogue
Three months later

"Oh, my gosh, seriously, you guys are *not* teenagers!"

Lucas glanced up and grinned at his fifteen-year-old daughter, Jasmine. He couldn't believe how much time had passed since the day she was born. Nearly sixteen now and just as much a beauty as her mother. She was also as stubborn as any of the Anderson males.

"I am simply giving your mother a kiss," he said and nuzzled Amy's neck.

"Honestly, I'll need therapy," Jasmine said with a roll of her eyes, but there was a sparkle in them, too. For all her protests, she lived in a very loving home, and she was a well-rounded and idealistic young woman. She just couldn't let her parents know that she thought their constant need to hold each other even after sixteen years was beautiful. Saying *ewwww* was more fun.

"You'll soon be sneaking off to kiss boys yourself, young lady," Amy said, making Lucas tense up.

"Over my dead body!"

"Oh, Lucas. Our baby girl is no longer a baby. If you'd quit scaring all her male friends, she might actually get her first kiss," said Amy, running a soothing hand over his arm, though it was doing nothing to soothe him.

"Jasmine's far too young to be kissing anyone," he stated emphatically.

"Oh, so you hadn't kissed anyone by the age of sixteen?" Amy challenged.

"That's beside the point," he said.

"I think I'll go kiss a boy right now just to show you both how gross you look doing it all the time, and in front of me," Jasmine said with a smirk.

"Good. I need someone to kill." Mark joined in the conversation as he entered the room.

"Hi, Uncle Mark. It's about time you got here. I can't wait to come spend the weekend with you and Aunt Emily," Jasmine said and launched herself at her favorite uncle.

"It's good to see you, squirt. What in the hell is this talk of you kissing boys?" he demanded, though his eyes were soft as he looked down at her. They had a close bond. Mark had a softer spot for Jasmine than any of the other nieces and nephews.

"I was just trying to prove a point to my parents about how disgusting it is to see old people

270

smooching all the time. Not that you'll help me, because you and Aunt Emily are just as bad. But, for some reason, it's just not as gross catching the two of you."

"That's because I'm so much younger and better-looking than your old stuffed shirt of a father," Mark said and puffed out his still-magnificent chest.

"You are still quite the looker, babe," Emily said, joining them and giving him a brief kiss.

"Ugh. I'm going to find Uncle Alex. At least *he* has some manners," Jasmine told them, then skipped away.

"Should I tell her that he's currently hiding in the closet with Jessica?" Mark said with laughter.

"Nah, let her face even more trauma when she finds them," Lucas answered.

Placing their arms around their wives, Lucas and Mark led them into the great room, where their huge family was gathering.

Over the past fifteen years, the Anderson family had certainly grown a lot larger. With Lucas marrying his beautiful wife Amy, and then Alex and Mark following in his steps, the clan had more than doubled in size.

When their Uncle George had come back to town with their four cousins, it had grown even more, especially as the cousins had married one by one, and then started having their own children.

The holidays were never quiet, and the home of their father, Joseph, was filled with love and laugher, just as he wanted it.

271

"Hey, Cousin, can you give me a hand? Isabelle is throwing a major fit, and you know how she adores you."

Lucas laughed at the panicked look on Austin's face. Isabelle, who was five years old now and an only child, was a holy terror. Lucas adored her.

"Of course. She just needs her Uncle Lucas," he said confidently

"Thank you," Austin said in relief. "I swore up and down to Kinsey that I had everything under control. I don't know how she manages to keep everything running so efficiently, but my hat's off to that woman," he said as the two of them walked out front, where Isabelle's impressive vocal cords could be heard echoing from the front driveway.

Two of the employees were standing guard at the vehicle, but both looked as if they'd rather be flayed alive than reach into the car and try to get the screaming child out.

"Why is she so upset?" Lucas asked as they approached.

"I forgot her blankie," Austin said, as if afraid the world would implode because Isabelle's favorite pink blankie had been left behind.

"Ooh, I see how much trouble you're in. It's a good thing Uncle Lucas can make it all better." Walking up to the large SUV, Lucas leaned in and smiled at a screaming Isabelle. "Hey, darling, did your daddy make you mad?"

She quieted as soon as she saw Lucas, and then the tears started in earnest as she looked pitifully up at him with her big blue eyes. She could already milk a situation for all it was worth.

"Daddy...for...forgot...my...blankie," she sniffled in between sobbing hiccups.

"I'm sorry, baby. Let Uncle Lucas take you inside, 'cause I have a surprise for you," he said.

She looked up at him with a bit of curiosity and her crying dimmed. Lucas could hear Austin sigh heavily behind him.

"Su...su...surprise?" she asked, still not sure whether she was willing to leave the car.

"Yes, surprise. But, only big girls get it." That was all it took. Because she was the youngest of all the cousins, Isabelle's major goal in life was to be a big girl.

Lucas knew that Grandma Katherine and Grandma Esther and all the children's aunts and moms had spent all year making them new quilts. They'd used pieces of their newborn clothes and nursery blankets, and other cherished fabrics. Their grandmothers wanted to give these gifts to each of them on Thanksgiving, not Christmas, when the abundance of toys would make the quilts seem less special.

The women had all put their hearts into the project, and Lucas had a feeling it was going to become a family tradition for any new members of the family to receive one the year they were born.

While Lucas calmed Isabelle and Mark hunted Alex down to offer help in the sitting room, their new cousins began arriving. The entire family was happy to meet new kinfolk, and knew that Joseph, George and Richard were particularly jubilant.

As they rounded the corner, Lucas bumped into someone he hadn't met yet.

"I'm sorry," he said as he brought up his hand to protect Isabelle's head.

"This house is huge, and I was admiring a painting, so wasn't paying attention. I'm Crew Storm," said the man, whose arm was around a petite blonde.

Lucas shifted Isabelle to his hip so he could shake Crew's hand.

"Lucas Anderson. I'm one of your many cousins," he replied.

"I've heard all about you, Lucas. It's a pleasure to finally put a face to the name. This is my fiancée, Haley Sutherland."

"Hello, Crew," Amy said as she joined them. "Haley, would you like to join us women in the library?"

Lucas beamed at his wife. She always had a friendly smile for everyone, and he knew she would welcome his new family with open arms.

Haley gave Amy a tentative smile as she released Crew's arm and followed Amy away.

"Congratulations, Cousin. She's beautiful," Lucas said and slapped him on the back. The two of them went to the playroom so they could hand off Isabelle to her grandmother and then go together for a cigar and a drink.

Meanwhile, Joseph, George and Richard sat in the den sipping cognac from crystal glasses as they enjoyed the warmth of the fire.

"Richard, I can't even tell you how thankful I am this year that we've discovered a new brother. You are a person I'd call friend even if you weren't blood," Joseph said, his voice choking just the slightest. He quickly took a sip from his glass and looked at the leaping flames.

"I couldn't be happier to know you. But I *have* decided to forgive my parents. What they did was wrong on so many levels, but they loved me, and I know I'm the man I am today because of the way they raised me. It saddens me to have missed the opportunity to meet my real parents, but I'll learn all about them through the both of you. Our kids will now get to know each other, and our grandkids will be close, as well."

"Speaking of grandkids, congratulations on the upcoming nuptials of Crew and Haley. That is wonderful. You may have your first grandbaby by Christmas next year," George said. "I wish our kids had gotten engaged without us having to push them."

"Oh, Crew needed a little push. I met Haley and fixed the drawing for her to get two weeks at Crew's resort," Richard said with a beaming smile.

"Brother, you are a man after our hearts. You *must* tell us what happened," Joseph said, leaning back. The three of them were roaring with laughter by the time Richard finished his tale.

"So now that you have one child married off, what are your plans for the other four?" Joseph asked, his eyes lit up.

"Well, a few months ago I met this real sweet girl who's graduating at the end of spring term with her bachelor's in biochemistry. She's going on for her master's in oceanography sciences, but she has the summer off, and she's fascinated by sunken treasures. It just so happens that my boy Ashton owns a boating business out of Seattle. I've given her a card and told her he'd be more than happy for some work."

"It sounds like she'll be too busy for a family," George stated as he took a puff from his cigar.

"Nonsense, Brother. She's such a sweet thing, and in need of a man to help her let down her hair. I think sparks are going to fly between the two of them."

"Well, then, we have some work to do," Joseph exclaimed, and he leaped from his chair. The thought of matchmaking again sent his blood pumping.

There was nothing like family — and finding true love for those you loved so dearly.

The three men walked from the room toward the warmth and laughter of their still-expanding clan. It was a new day — and the sun continued to shine for the Andersons.

The End

Want to read more about The Lost
Andersons?
*Go to MelodyAnne.com, and add your email
address to the newsletter signup.
We'll email you whenever Melody Anne
releases a new book.*

The next book in the Lost Andersons Series, **Hidden Treasure – Coming Soon.** In the meantime, catch up with the characters in one of Melody's other series listed in the beginning of this book. Here's a sneak peak of The Tycoon's Revenge, available now.

Melody Anne Background

NYT and USA Today Best Selling Author Melody Anne has written the popular series, Billionaire Bachelors, Surrender Series and Baby for the Billionaire. She also has a Young Adult Series in high demand; Midnight Fire, Midnight Moon and Midnight Storm - Rise of the Dark Angel.

As an aspiring author, she wrote for years, then became published in 2011. Holding a Bachelor's Degree in business, she loves to write about strong, powerful, businessmen and the corporate world.

When Melody isn't writing, she cultivates strong bonds with her family and relatives and enjoys time spent with them as well as her friends, and beloved pets. A country girl at heart, she loves the small town and strong community she lives in and is involved in many community projects.

See Melody's Website at: www.melodyanne.com. She makes it a point to respond to all her fans. You can also join her on facebook at: www.facebook.com/melodyanneauthor, or at twitter: @authmelodyanne.

She looks forward to hearing from you and thanks you for your continued interest in her stories.

Printed in Great Britain
by Amazon.co.uk, Ltd.,
Marston Gate.